SWEET VALLEY TWINS
AND FRIENDS

Booster
Boycott

◇

Written by
Jamie Suzanne

Created by
FRANCINE PASCAL

A BANTAM SKYLARK BOOK
NEW YORK · TORONTO · LONDON · SYDNEY · AUCKLAND

RL 4, 008–012

BOOSTER BOYCOTT
A Bantam Skylark Book / September 1991

*Sweet Valley High® and Sweet Valley Twins and Friends are
trademarks of Francine Pascal*

Conceived by Francine Pascal

*Produced by Daniel Weiss Associates, Inc.
33 West 17th Street
New York, NY 10011*

Cover art by James Mathewuse

*Skylark Books is a registered trademark of Bantam Books, a division of
Bantam Doubleday Dell Publishing Group, Inc.
Registered in U.S. Patent and Trademark Office and elsewhere.*

ISBN 0-553-15933-X

Published simultaneously in the United States and Canada

---

*Bantam Books are published by Bantam Books, a division of Bantam Dou-
bleday Dell Publishing Group, Inc. Its trademark, consisting of the words
"Bantam Books" and the portrayal of a rooster, is Registered in U.S.
Patent and Trademark Office and in other countries. Marca Registrada.
Bantam Books, 666 Fifth Avenue, New York, New York 10103.*

PRINTED IN THE UNITED STATES OF AMERICA

OPM   0 9 8 7 6 5 4 3 2 1

Booster Boycott

One

◇

"I can't walk home with you today," Jessica Wakefield told her twin sister one Monday after school. "Tell Mom I may be home late. We're having another emergency Boosters meeting, and it might be extra long."

Elizabeth Wakefield smiled at her sister. "You guys sure are practicing hard for that competition! I'm proud of you." The Southern California Middle School Cheering Championship was in three weeks, and Sweet Valley Middle School was going to host it for the first time. In fact, it would be the first competition ever for the Boosters, Sweet Valley Middle School's cheering squad.

"Actually, this meeting has to do with Winston Egbert," Jessica said.

"Winston?" Elizabeth repeated. "What does Winston have to do with the Boosters?"

"Nothing, and it's going to stay that way! Believe it or not, that scrawny nerd actually wants to try out for the Boosters."

Elizabeth laughed. "Are you sure about this, Jess? Why would Winston Egbert want to be a Booster?"

"Because he's insane," Jessica answered. "That's the only reason I can think of."

"It's got to be some kind of joke," Lila Fowler said as she came up behind the twins. "He's actually coming to our practice this afternoon. Winston asked Janet what time he should stop by to talk about joining." Lila flipped her long brown hair over her shoulder. "She told him to come by around a quarter after *never!*"

"Maybe he's serious," Elizabeth said.

Jessica groaned. "We're talking about the Boosters, Elizabeth! Cheerleaders are *girls*, not geeky guys. Can you picture Winston twirling a baton and wearing a skirt?"

Jessica wasn't surprised when her twin scowled. *Elizabeth just doesn't understand how important cheerleading is*, she thought.

But there were a lot of things Jessica didn't understand about Elizabeth either. The two girls had such different personalities and interests that it was sometimes hard to believe they were identical twins. Physically, they were perfect copies of each other, right down to the tiny dimple in their left cheek. Both girls had long golden hair and sparkling blue-green eyes, and they wore exactly the same size clothes.

But that was where the similarities ended. Elizabeth was the more responsible, serious twin. A hard-working student, she loved to write and hoped someday to become a professional journalist. She was very proud of her position as editor of *The Sweet Valley Sixers*, the sixth-grade newspaper. Still, as busy as she was, Elizabeth always had time for her friends.

That included Jessica, who often relied on her sister to bail her out of tough situations. Jessica was more carefree than Elizabeth. She was a member of the Unicorns, a group of girls who thought they were the prettiest and most popular at school—girls Elizabeth had nicknamed "The Snob Squad." They always wore something purple, the color of royalty, to remind everyone that they were special. Unicorn meetings always involved the same subjects—boys, movie stars, the latest fashions, or the newest makeup tips. The Unicorns had started the Boosters. In fact, there was only one non-Unicorn on the Boosters—Amy Sutton, who was also Elizabeth's closest friend.

"Let's go, Jess!" Lila tugged at Jessica's arm. "We're late already!"

By the time Jessica and Lila arrived at the gym, most of the other Boosters were there.

"*There* you are!" Janet Howell shouted. Janet, an eighth grader, was the president of the Unicorns. "Hurry up. We need to decide what to do about Winston."

Lila and Jessica joined the other girls on the bleachers. "So it's true?" Lila asked. "Winston really wants to join the Boosters?"

Janet nodded. "He says that he's coming to the meeting this afternoon!"

Amy Sutton cleared her throat. "Why don't we let him try out?"

"Why would we want to do a thing like that?" Jessica snapped.

"It might be neat to have a guy on the squad," Amy continued. "It might even help our chances in the championship." She shrugged. "After all, we could *use* some help."

Jessica glared at Amy. "Our cheers are just fine the way they are!"

"It couldn't hurt to just *listen* to Winston, though, could it?" Grace Oliver asked. Grace, a tiny sixth grader, had long, silky black hair and dark eyes.

"Whose side are you on, Grace?" Janet cried in annoyance.

Grace looked down at her lap. *"Our* side," she said weakly. "I just thought—"

As Grace spoke the gym door swung open. Winston Egbert entered the gym, cradling a tower of books in his arms. The stack was so tall that the top book was tucked right under his chin. "Is this the Boosters meeting?" he asked from behind the books.

"Good guess, Sherlock!" Janet answered, and the rest of the group giggled.

Winston headed for the bleachers and carefully set down his pile of books.

"I think you're in the wrong place," Jessica said. "You must be looking for the science club."

"Or the Future Geeks of America meeting," Lila added.

Winston's ears grew scarlet. "You all probably know why I'm here," he began. "And you probably think I'm crazy, b-but I'd appreciate it if you'd just let me present my case."

"Give it up, Winston," yelled Tamara Chase, an eighth grader.

"Come on, Tamara," Janet scolded, trying not to grin. "Let's hear what Winston has to say. After all, I could use a good laugh!" Again, the girls giggled loudly.

"Go ahead, Winston," Amy Sutton urged. "I'm listening."

Winston looked at Amy gratefully. "All I'm asking for is a chance to try out. I think I could really help the squad."

"What's the matter with the squad?" Janet demanded, taking a step closer to Winston.

Winston backed up a step. "Nothing," he said quickly. "But with a guy on the squad you could add all kinds of new routines. And most high school cheering squads are coed."

Kimberly Haver, a seventh grader, spoke up. "Are you saying we should perform with a boy at our first competition? We'd all die of humiliation!"

"Besides, Winston, what do you think we do when we're not practicing cheers?" Janet asked.

Winston shrugged helplessly. "I don't know. Warmup exercises? Baton drills?"

"Wrong." Janet crossed her arms over her chest. "We talk about *guys*. Now how are we going to talk about guys with a guy around?"

"But that's discrimination!" Winston protested weakly.

"Give me a break!" Jessica moaned. "Everybody knows there's no such thing as discrimination against boys!"

"What a joke!" Ellen Riteman chimed in.

"Why don't you just let me show you what I can do?" Winston said.

"Why don't you go join the baseball team?" Janet responded.

"Come on, you guys," Amy said. "Why not let him try out? What can it hurt?"

"It can hurt our reputations!" Janet argued. "We'll be the laughingstocks of the school."

"The Boosters are the most popular girls in school," Ellen added. "How are we going to look cheering with Winston Egbert?"

"If you think having Winston on the Boosters will ruin your popularity, Ellen, then you're probably not very popular to begin with!" Amy shot back.

"See what's happening?" Janet said to Winston. "You've only been here a few minutes and already you've disrupted everything. And we have less than three weeks before our big competition."

Winston stared down at his sneakers. After a few tense moments, he picked up his pile of science books and slowly walked away.

As he reached for the handle of the door, he lost his grip on the books, and they tumbled to the floor in a heap. The crash echoed in the almost-empty gymnasium. While the Boosters giggled, Winston knelt down and grabbed his books, his face turning the color of a ripe tomato. But when he stood up he turned around and glared at the Boosters, his mouth set in a determined line. "I won't give up without a fight," he said, and disappeared out the door.

"Good riddance," Lila muttered.

"Well, at least that's over with," Janet said, sounding relieved. "Victory!"

Jessica watched the door close behind Winston. Something in his voice made Jessica think the Boosters hadn't seen the last of Winston Egbert.

Two

◇

Winston paused in the empty hallway outside the gym. Through the doors, he could hear the Boosters as they began practicing a cheer.

I won't give up without a fight. Had he *really* just said that to a roomful of Boosters?

I must be braver than I thought, he told himself as he headed down the hallway. *Braver—or maybe dumber.*

"Hey, Egbert! What's up?" Todd Wilkins came up behind Winston and playfully slapped him on the back.

Winston wobbled, then passed a few books to Todd. "Help me out with these. I've already dropped them once."

Todd examined the books. "Are these for

your science project? I haven't even thought about mine yet."

Winston nodded as Todd walked toward the gym. "If you're on your way to play some basketball, the gym's already taken."

"Oh yeah, I forgot. Coach Cassels told me the gym's off-limits while the Boosters practice." Todd rolled his eyes and turned away from the gym. "Like cheerleading is more important than basketball! What were you doing in there, anyway?"

Winston strode down the front steps two at a time. "You wouldn't believe me if I told you."

Todd paused at the bottom of the steps. "You were asking Lila Fowler to go out with you?" he joked.

Winston couldn't help but laugh. "You're not even warm."

"I know!" Todd said, his eyes lighting up. "You were trying out for the squad!"

Winston shifted uncomfortably. It was obvious that Todd thought the idea was hilarious. But Todd—and everyone else in school—was going to hear about Winston's attempt to audition for the Boosters soon enough.

"Believe it or not, that *is* why I was in the gym," Winston admitted. He hesitated, waiting for Todd's response. Todd was his friend, but Winston wouldn't have blamed him for laughing.

But Todd didn't laugh. "You're serious?" he asked.

"Yep," Winston replied, trying to sound casual.

"But *why?*"

"A lot of reasons," Winston answered. "I . . . um . . . I like gymnastics a lot. The Boosters could really use some help in the cheering competition. And . . . well, uh, it seems like a good way to meet girls."

Todd grinned. "It's a great way to meet girls!"

Winston smiled back. He felt relieved to have told Todd. Maybe Todd could even give him a few pointers on talking to girls, he figured. He could use all the help he could get.

"It doesn't look like I'll be getting to know any of the Boosters, though," Winston admitted. "They weren't very thrilled at the idea of me trying out. In fact, they pretty much threw me out of the gym!"

"Where there's a will, there's a way," Todd replied. "But the Boosters can be pretty tough when they want to be."

"I can handle them," Winston said, trying to believe his own words.

"I'm sure you can," Todd agreed. "There's only one little problem," he added with a sly grin.

"What's that?"

"Do they make those little cheerleader skirts in your size?"

* * *

Elizabeth was on her way to her second-period class Tuesday morning when she spotted Winston digging through his locker.

"Winston!" she called. "Wait up!"

Winston looked up and grinned. "Hey, Elizabeth. What's up?"

Elizabeth laughed. "I was just going to ask you that question!"

Winston smiled and then looked down at his feet. "You mean the Boosters thing. I guess Jessica told you all about what happened at the practice yesterday."

Elizabeth nodded sympathetically. It was all Jessica had talked about the night before—and she hadn't had anything nice to say.

"I'm not sure I understand why you want to join the Boosters," she said. "I mean, they're pretty snobby—except for Amy—and they're going to give you a really hard time." She leaned against the locker next to Winston's. "From what Amy's told me, they can make your life miserable if you're not a Unicorn."

"Well, I'm never going to be a Unicorn," Winston said. "To begin with, I don't own a single piece of purple clothing!"

Elizabeth laughed, but Winston's brown eyes turned serious.

"The reason I want to join the Boosters," he

said after a pause, "is probably the same reason Amy wanted to join. She may not have much in common with the other girls on the squad, but she's the best baton twirler of the bunch and she wanted a chance to put her talent to good use. And—" Winston hesitated, and his ears began to turn pink, "I'm not a bad gymnast."

Elizabeth was genuinely surprised. She had known Winston since they were little kids, and he had never mentioned this before. "I didn't know you were a gymnast!"

"Well, I'm not ready for the Olympics. But last summer I took gymnastics lessons, and I've been practicing ever since. I've watched some coed high school and college cheering squads, and the moves they do are amazing." He shut his locker. "If I could show the Boosters what I can do, I know they'd change their minds about letting me on the squad."

"And you're sure you could stand to be surrounded by that many Unicorns?" Elizabeth teased.

"Amy would be there," Winston reminded her. "And besides," he added with a shy smile, "the Unicorns aren't all bad."

"Well, I'll do my best to convince Jessica that you're right," Elizabeth promised. "I think the idea of a coed cheerleading squad is great."

"You do?"

Elizabeth nodded. "I'll bet I'm not the only

one, either. I'm sure plenty. of students would agree with me. Guys *and* girls."

Winston's eyes lit up. "That's it, Elizabeth!" he yelled. "You're a genius!"

"What did I say?"

"It's a great idea! The Boosters will *have* to let me try out! Thanks a million!"

Elizabeth stood dumbfounded, watching as Winston sprinted down the hallway. "You're welcome," she said, shrugging. "I just wish I knew what I did."

"What's Winston Egbert doing over there?" Amy asked at lunchtime as she and Elizabeth took their seats in the cafeteria.

Elizabeth followed Amy's gaze. Winston was standing next to a table of seventh-grade girls, passing around a clipboard.

"Looks like he's handing around a petition," Belinda Layton said as she joined them.

"I hope it's a petition for better lunches," Amy said. She poked her fork at the gray mass on her plate. "What is this stuff, anyway? Leftovers from somebody's science project?"

"Speaking of science projects," Belinda said, "have you decided what you're going to do for yours, Amy?"

"Nope, but I know it's going to involve frogs," Amy answered as she buttered her roll.

"Frogs?" Belinda repeated.

"We've got tons of them in our backyard." Amy frowned at her lunch tray. "Maybe I'll experiment with their diet. I'll feed them mystery meat from the cafeteria and see how long they survive. What do you think, Elizabeth?"

"What?" Elizabeth asked, obviously distracted.

"About my frogs."

"Sorry, Amy," Elizabeth said. "I was watching Winston. I'll bet he's going to give the Boosters a petition demanding that they let him try out."

"Good for him," Belinda said. "I'll sign it." Belinda, who was a member of the Unicorns, was the most respected athlete in school. She was also the only girl on the Little League softball team.

"Me, too," Amy agreed. "But I'm not sure it'll convince Janet and the rest of them."

"I think it's a terrific idea," Elizabeth said. "I'm sure this isn't easy for Winston. He's usually pretty shy. Joining the Boosters must really mean a lot to him."

"I'm not sure why he would want to, after the way they treated him yesterday," Amy said.

A few minutes later, Winston arrived at the girls' table. "See?" he said to Elizabeth, holding up the clipboard for them to examine. "Three signatures already!" He passed the petition to Elizabeth. "I'd be honored if you'd sign. After all, it *was* your idea."

"I never said anything about starting a petition."

"No, but you reminded me that I could probably find a lot of support from all the non-Unicorns out there."

Elizabeth read the top of the petition out loud. " 'We, the undersigned, in the interest of fairness, justice, and equality of the sexes, do hereby declare that Winston X. Egbert be allowed the chance to try out for the Boosters.' " She looked up at Winston and grinned. "Nice job."

"What's the X stand for?" Amy asked.

"Xavier," Winston said under his breath, coloring slightly.

"Impressive," Amy said. She reached for the petition. "I want to sign next. And I'm going to put my name in extra-large letters so all the other Boosters can see it."

"I'm next," Belinda volunteered. "I know how hard it is to do something different. I'd like to be the first Unicorn to sign your petition!"

Winston sat down in the chair opposite Elizabeth. "I hope this works," he said nervously, glancing over at the Unicorner, where most of the Unicorns sat at lunch.

"Me, too," Elizabeth replied. "You can count on me to do whatever I can to help."

Winston smiled gratefully. "Thanks, Elizabeth."

Just then Elizabeth looked up to see Todd Wilkins and Ken Matthews approaching. The two boys leaned against the table. "What's everybody signing?" Todd asked.

"Winston is circulating a petition," Elizabeth explained. She moved over a seat so that Todd could sit next to her.

"What kind of petition?" Ken asked as he sat down next to Amy.

"Does this have anything to do with you trying to join the Boosters?" Todd asked Winston.

Winston nodded. "I'm hoping this will convince them to let me audition for the squad."

"So what is it you want to be?" Ken asked, grinning. "The guy who gets to spray their hair between cheers?"

"He wants to be a cheerleader," Elizabeth said in Winston's defense. "And I'm sure he'll be a very good one!" She reached for the petition. "Here," she said, passing the clipboard to Todd. "I'm sure you two will want to sign."

"That's OK, guys," Winston said, a little sheepishly. "You don't have to if you don't want to."

Todd smiled. "Like I told you, anybody willing to stand up to the Unicorns has my vote, Winston!" He signed his name to the petition and handed it to Ken, who also signed.

"Great!" Winston said happily. "Thanks a lot."

"Sure," Todd said as he pushed back his chair

and stood. "Good luck with your petition." He turned to Elizabeth. "See you later?"

Elizabeth nodded, smiling. Winston stood up, too. "Well, cross your fingers," he said. "I'm off to see the Wicked Witch of the West."

"You must mean Janet," Amy said, giggling. "You're not actually going to ask the Unicorns to sign your petition, are you?"

"The more the merrier," Winston replied lightly, but when he looked over at the Unicorner he swallowed hard.

"We'll come with you," Elizabeth volunteered. "For moral support."

Winston headed for the Unicorns' table with Elizabeth, Amy, and Belinda close by.

"Hello," Winston said as all the Unicorns turned to stare at him. "I—"

"This table is reserved for Unicorns," Janet interrupted haughtily.

Color crept into Winston's cheeks. "I thought you might be interested in this," he said, timidly placing his petition in front of Janet.

Three

◇

Janet stared at the paper as though she were afraid to touch it.

"What is it?" Grace finally asked, smiling at Winston.

"It's a petition asking that I be allowed to try out for a spot on your illustrious cheerleading squad," Winston answered, as color traveled up his face and reached the tips of his ears.

"How dare you insult the Boosters!" Kimberly Haver cried self-righteously, pushing aside her sandwich.

"Kimberly," Janet said in a low whisper, "I think *illustrious* is a compliment."

"It is," Winston assured them. "I really admire the Boosters." He smiled shyly at Grace. "Why else would I want to join?"

"How many names are on this thing, anyway?" Janet asked frostily.

"Eight," Winston answered. "But I just started collecting signatures."

"Big deal," Lila scoffed. "So he got his friends to sign."

"I signed," Elizabeth said loudly.

"So did I," Amy chimed in.

Janet looked at Amy with disgust. "Amy, you didn't!"

"Yes, I did!"

"What do you expect?" Janet said. "This is what we get for having an outsider on the squad. We should have kept the Boosters strictly Unicorns when we started out."

"Amy is the best twirler of you all," Belinda pointed out. "You had to let her on the squad! And besides, I signed, too!"

"Some Unicorn you are," Lila sneered.

"Belinda! Don't you see why we can't let a guy on?" Janet asked. "We have to have some standards!"

"I think Belinda and Amy are right," said Mandy Miller, the newest sixth-grade Unicorn.

Janet sighed. "Did I ask for your opinion, Mandy?"

"Suppose Winston was a better gymnast than the rest of you," Elizabeth said. "What then?"

"Oh, come on, Elizabeth," Jessica said.

Janet pounded her fist on the table. "I don't care if Winston is the best gymnast in California. I don't care if he's the champion of the world! He's not Booster material!"

Winston cleared his throat. "How many signatures would it take to convince you to let me try out?"

Janet glanced at the other Unicorns. "Oh, I don't know," she replied, the corners of her mouth curving into a smile. "How about, say, one hundred?"

Winston gulped. "That's practically the whole sixth grade!"

Janet grinned deviously. "So get some seventh and eighth graders."

Winston reached for the petition. "All right," he said, "maybe I will."

"Dream on," Tamara Chase said as the girls burst into laughter.

Winston handed the petition to Jessica. "Would you like to be the first Unicorn at your table to sign?"

"Winston," Jessica said with a long-suffering sigh, "what planet are you from anyway?"

Winston cast a pleading look at Grace. "Come on, Grace," he urged gently, "how about you?"

Grace pulled at a few strands of her hair nervously. "Sure," she said, her voice quaking.

"Grace!" Janet exclaimed. "Have you lost your mind?"

"I only thought—"

"Well, stop thinking!" Janet commanded.

"Traitor," Lila muttered.

"Benedict Armhole," Ellen added.

"That's *Arnold*, Ellen," Janet snapped.

"Come on, Grace," Winston urged. He passed her the clipboard. "It can't hurt you to sign."

"No, but *I* can," Janet threatened, jerking the petition out of Grace's hands. She motioned to the rest of the group. "C'mon, everybody. Let's go outside and practice some cheers!"

The Unicorns followed Janet out of the lunchroom. "Sorry," Grace said softly as she passed by Winston.

Winston watched the Unicorns file out, a wistful look on his face. "Well," he said at last, turning to Elizabeth, "eight down, ninety-two to go."

At Boosters practice that afternoon, nothing seemed to go right.

As usual, no one could agree on anything. Jessica and Lila each had invented new cheers, and they spent the first twenty minutes of practice arguing over which cheer was better. Tamara was tired of being stuck in the back row just because she was taller than everyone else. And Amy was still angry over the way Janet had treated Winston in the lunchroom.

When the human pyramid they had been

practicing collapsed for the sixth time that afternoon, everyone finally agreed on one thing: It was time to take a break.

"You call yourselves cheerleaders?" Janet yelled, pacing across the shiny gym floor. "You're a disgrace to the cheerleading tradition."

"What tradition?" Lila asked. She was sprawled across a bottom bleacher. "We just organized the Boosters this year."

"Well, there won't be a Boosters next year if we flop at the championship," Janet said icily. "It's an honor to have our school host the competition—especially since this will be the first time the Boosters have participated. There will be schools here from all over southern California. Not to mention all our friends and families and teachers and"—she paused for effect—"boyfriends." Janet looked at them meaningfully. "You don't want us to look like losers, do you?"

Nobody answered. "Is *anybody* listening to me?" Janet demanded irritably. "Tamara?"

"All I'm asking is to be in the front for one lousy cheer," Tamara grumbled.

"We've been through this already," Janet groaned. "You have to be in back with Amy and Kimberly. You're the tallest."

Tamara made a face.

"Does anyone have anything *positive* to contribute?" Janet wailed.

Jessica, who was sitting on the gym floor reading a magazine, raised her hand. "I have something positive to say."

Janet sighed. "Finally!"

"I would like to say that my new cheer is far superior to Lila's."

"It is not," Lila snapped.

"Is too," Jessica said.

"You both sound like five-year-olds," Amy said grouchily. "And anyway, *both* cheers are stupid."

"What's wrong with my cheer?" Lila demanded.

" 'Go Sweet Valley—please don't dally' " is the dumbest cheer I've ever heard," Amy said.

"She's right, Lila," Jessica agreed.

"You try to rhyme something with *valley*," Lila said, pouting. "It isn't easy."

"And yours, Jessica," Amy continued. "I think ending it with a pyramid is a fine idea, but why should you be on top?"

"Because I invented the cheer," Jessica said, sticking out her chin defiantly.

"But Grace is the smallest one on the squad, and I'm not sure my back can take the strain of having you on top."

Jessica gave Amy a withering stare.

"Do you have anything to add, Grace?" Janet asked.

Grace looked up from the notepad she was holding. "Did someone call my name?" she asked.

"What are you doing, anyway?" Janet said impatiently.

"Just doodling," Grace replied. "Since we're not getting much done—"

Ms. Langberg, the P.E. teacher and the Boosters' advisor, approached the girls. "Am I interrupting anything, ladies?"

"Um, no, Ms. Langberg," Janet said quickly. "We were just taking a little break."

"So I see." Ms. Langberg scanned the group. "If you plan to do well at the championship, I hope I see more practicing and fewer breaks."

"Yes, Ms. Langberg," Janet said sheepishly.

"I'd hate to think you bought those new uniforms for nothing," she added. The Boosters had purchased, with their own money, brand-new uniforms for the competition. They were short purple-and-white pleated skirts and V-necked white sweaters with the letters *SV* on them. Actually, the school colors were blue and white, but the Unicorns had cheated by picking out a purple so dark it could almost pass for navy blue. After all, purple *was* their official color.

As soon as Ms. Langberg was gone, Janet exploded. "I *told* you we have to work harder!"

"We just had a practice yesterday," Lila pointed out sullenly. "Lighten up, Janet."

"But most of that practice was taken up by Winston," Jessica complained.

"That's the problem, if you ask me," Kimberly said as she idly rolled her baton between her fingers. "None of us can concentrate because of creepy Winston Egbert."

"I don't think our problems have anything to do with Winston," Amy said loudly.

"Me, either," Grace chimed in.

"Well, I think Kimberly's right," Jessica argued. "I know he's ruined *my* concentration."

"Who can concentrate when we know that at any minute the Boosters could be invaded by a nerdy guy?" Lila said dramatically.

"We need to solve this problem once and for all," Janet said. "What if Winston doesn't leave us alone? He could destroy our chances of winning the championship."

"Personally, I think *we're* our own worst enemy," Amy said dryly. "I'm sure we can mess up our chances without any help from Winston."

Janet ignored Amy. "We all know Winston is just trying to get attention, right? He doesn't really want to be a Booster. What we need to do is tell everyone the truth: that Winston's petition is a fake. He's just making fun of us and the proud tradition of cheerleading. And we're not going to put up with it, right?"

"Right!" Jessica cried. It was the first time she had agreed with Janet all afternoon.

"Then, once we're rid of Winston, we can get down to some serious practicing," Janet concluded. She checked her watch. "Well, I think that's enough for today, don't you?"

"Practice is over?" Amy cried. "But we haven't accomplished anything!"

"Sure we have," Jessica said, smiling slyly. "We've decided how to get rid of Winston."

Four

◇

Wednesday morning Jessica and Lila had just stepped out of homeroom when they noticed Winston showing his petition to two sixth graders.

"Let's put our plan into effect," Jessica whispered to Lila. "Let's go tell them the truth about Winston."

"But, Jess," Lila protested, "that's just Leslie Forsythe and Randy Mason. Who cares what they think?"

"I know who they are." Jessica tapped her foot impatiently. "But didn't you hear everyone in homeroom talking about Winston? This thing is getting out of control, Lila. I'll bet you half the kids in homeroom were in favor of letting Winston try out."

Lila looked worried. "You may be right. Someone told me Mrs. Arnette heard about Winston yesterday and announced she was going to use him as a discussion topic in social studies." She shrugged. "Something about sex discrimination."

"Great. *We're* the ones being discriminated against, and Winston gets to be a social studies topic. He's a guy! He doesn't have to worry about equality. He's already equal!" Jessica nodded toward Leslie and Randy. "Come on. Let's give them our side of the story."

As the girls approached, Leslie and Randy were carefully scrutinizing the petition. Randy was one of the smartest boys in sixth grade and also one of the shyest. Although he had been elected class president, the Unicorns considered him definite geek material. The same went for Leslie, a scrawny girl who seemed to have a perpetually runny nose.

"Hi, guys," Jessica said, sauntering up to Leslie with a smile pasted on her face. She cast an admiring glance at Leslie's plain blue dress. "What a great outfit, Leslie."

Leslie's mouth dropped open in surprise. "Thanks, Jessica," she said as she pulled a crumpled tissue from her backpack.

"What have you got there, Randy?" Lila drawled, edging a little closer to him.

Randy stole a shy glance at Lila. "It's a petition to—"

"They know what it is, Randy," Winston assured him. "Have you guys decided to add your names?"

"You're not actually going to sign that thing, are you?" Jessica asked Leslie, ignoring Winston entirely.

Leslie sniffled. "Well, actually, I was going to—"

"We girls have to stick together, Leslie," Lila interrupted. "Don't you agree?"

Leslie's eyes darted from Lila to Winston. "Well, sure," she answered hesitantly. "But couldn't you just let him try out? It couldn't hurt."

"Of course it could hurt," Jessica argued. "It would destroy the Boosters' morale, right before a major competition. Don't you have any school spirit, Leslie?"

Leslie shuffled her feet. "Well, kind of."

Randy spoke up. "Excuse me, but I don't see this as a question of school spirit. Fundamentally, it comes down to a matter of injustice."

"You're so right, Randy," Lila cooed, tossing her hair back over her shoulder. She shook her finger at Winston. "We all know that your petition is a fake. You're just trying to make fun of cheerleading. And you'd better apologize to the Boosters this instant."

"You don't understand, Lila. It's Winston who's been treated unfairly. The Boosters should be apologizing to him," Randy said.

"Oh, *please!*" Lila groaned.

Winston smiled gratefully at Randy. "We guys have to stick together, Lila," Winston said, imitating her tone. "Don't you agree?"

"If you ever run for class president again, Randy Mason, you've lost my vote!" Lila growled.

Randy grinned at Winston. "I'll keep that in mind," he said, signing his name on the petition.

Jessica turned all her charm on Leslie. "At least Leslie knows better than to sign that stupid petition," she said. "After all, who would you rather have as friends, Leslie? The Boosters—who are, after all, the most popular girls in school—or Winston Egbert?"

"Who is, after all," Winston said with a grin, "definitely *not* one of the most popular girls in school."

Jessica could tell by Leslie's awed expression that she nearly had her hooked. "Think about it, Leslie. Wouldn't you like to have the Boosters as friends?"

Leslie pursed her lips. "What do you mean by *friends*, exactly?"

Jessica glanced at Lila in annoyance. She didn't want to commit to anything major, after all. Not with Leslie, the Sniffle Queen of Sweet Valley.

"Well, take right now, for instance," Jessica said. "Normally, Lila and I would have walked right by you in the hallway without saying a word, right?"

"Right."

"So, if you refuse to sign that petition, from now on Lila and I will promise to say hi to you whenever we see you."

"Only in the halls," Lila added quickly.

"Or we might just wave," Jessica said as an afterthought.

"Boy, Leslie," Winston said with an exaggerated shake of his head, "that's a mighty tempting offer. I'll understand if you want to go for it."

Leslie stood a little straighter and flashed Winston a confident smile. "Thanks, anyway," she said to Jessica. "But I'd rather have Winston say hi to me in the halls. Can I borrow your pen, Randy?"

"Score two more in the fight for equality!" Winston said happily.

"Come on, Lila," Jessica said. "So what if he gets all the nerds to sign? He still doesn't have a prayer."

Leslie looked up from the paper she had just signed. "There are a lot more nerds in this school than there are Unicorns."

Jessica sighed and turned to leave, only to run into Elizabeth and Amy.

"What's going on, Jess?" Elizabeth teased. "Were you and Lila signing Winston's petition?"

"He doesn't need their signatures," Amy said. "He's got plenty without them."

Jessica put her hands on her hips. "You'd think I could count on my own twin to support me! Why are you on Winston's side, anyway?"

"Because he's right," Elizabeth answered.

Lila made a face. "Since when are you so buddy-buddy with Winston, Elizabeth?" She nudged Jessica. "Maybe there's something going on between them, Jess!"

"I *thought* Todd was her boyfriend," Jessica said, "but now I'm beginning to wonder."

Jessica and Lila walked off together, leaving Elizabeth and Amy behind. "How ridiculous," Elizabeth said. "Jessica knows Winston and I are only friends. Is there some law against guys and girls being friends?"

"One hundred and one . . . one hundred and two . . ." Winston stood outside the crowded cafeteria at lunchtime counting the names on his petition. It was hard to believe, but one hundred and seven people had signed his petition! Some of them were friends, but most were strangers, or near-strangers. That morning he had actually gone up to eighth-grade girls he'd never met before and pleaded his case. And miraculously, most of them had agreed to sign his petition! One of the girls had said she thought he would make a cute addition to the squad! *Imagine*, he thought, *Winston X. Egbert, a cute addition*.

"How's the petition going, Winston?" Todd asked as he headed toward the lunchroom. "I'd sign again, but I think that's illegal."

"You don't need to," Winston said proudly. "I've got over one hundred signatures."

"Wow. You must be a great salesman." Todd opened the cafeteria door. "Are you coming?"

"In a minute," Winston answered. "I want to count signatures one more time, just to be sure I'm right."

Winston leaned against the wall, scanning the scribbled names on the page. Maybe Todd was right. He wasn't a bad salesman. Once he had gotten the hang of it, he'd found that talking to people wasn't so hard after all. The more he joked with them, the less awkward it felt. That morning when he was asking eighth graders to sign, he hadn't even blushed.

"One, two . . ." Winston began counting again, a broad grin on his face.

"So how's our anti-Winston campaign coming?" Janet asked at lunch.

Jessica took a bite of her carrot. She didn't feel like admitting that she and Lila hadn't been able to convert Leslie and Randy.

"In social studies Mrs. Arnette made us discuss sex discrimination," Ellen said. "I tried to explain to everybody that Winston is just trying to make fun of cheerleaders, but the Hairnet said I was wrong. Anyway," Ellen continued, "we took a vote on whether or not he should get to try out, and Winston actually won, thirteen to ten!"

Grace began to peel an orange. "I saw Winston in the hall passing around his petition this morning," she said.

"You didn't sign it, did you?" Janet demanded.

Grace looked Janet straight in the eye. "Yes, actually, I did. I don't see what's wrong with letting him try out."

"You're as bad as Amy Sutton!" Jessica said.

"Thanks, Jess," Grace said, smiling slightly. "I take that as a compliment."

"She's *worse* than Amy!" Lila said. "Grace is a Unicorn! Unicorns are supposed to stick together!"

"Well, it doesn't matter," Jessica said. "One traitor won't help Winston very much."

"Make that *two* traitors," Mandy said, smiling at Grace. "I signed this morning, too."

Jessica groaned. "Still, I'm sure Winston

doesn't have that many signatures. I'll bet he's got maybe a dozen at the most."

"Wrong, Jessica."

Jessica looked behind her to discover Winston standing there with his clipboard in his hand.

"I have a few more signatures than that," Winston said brightly. "Would anyone like to guess how many? The closest guess wins an all-expense-paid date with none other than me."

Grace giggled, and Winston cast her a smile. Jessica sighed disgustedly.

"I'd rather have a math test," Janet muttered.

"Or a cavity filled," Lila chimed in.

"I'm flattered!" Winston said. "I guess I'll just go ahead and tell you."

Jessica rolled her eyes. She had never seen Winston act so confident. It was truly annoying.

Winston presented the petition to Janet with a flourish. "One hundred and seven names," Winston announced proudly. "How about that, Janet?"

Janet looked around the table, then down at the long list of names. "Hmm," she murmured, shifting in her chair, "I guess this *does* sort of change things."

Winston scanned her face anxiously.

"I must say I'm impressed, Winston," Janet admitted. She carefully folded the petition and placed in into her backpack while the others watched in horrified silence. "I promise to talk to Ms. Langberg about this. It's the least I can do, after all the hard work you've put into this petition."

"But Janet!" Jessica said, unable to believe her own ears. *Janet* was actually giving in to Winston's demands?

"I don't have any choice, Jessica," Janet said. "I have to be fair."

Winston grinned from ear to ear. "Thanks, Janet," he said excitedly. "I promise you won't regret this!"

Jessica watched as Winston raced off to tell Elizabeth the good news. "Janet!" she growled, "what's the matter with you?"

"How could you do this?" Tamara wailed.

"Do what?" Janet asked, smiling serenely. "I haven't done a thing." She leaned forward and added in a low whisper to Jessica and Lila, "Emergency Unicorn meeting this afternoon at Casey's! The future of the Boosters is at stake!"

Five

◇

"Are you going to tell us what this is about?" Jessica demanded as the Unicorns crowded into their favorite booth at Casey's. Casey's Place, an old-fashioned ice cream parlor at the Valley Mall, was a regular hangout of the Unicorns.

"In a minute, in a minute," Janet answered casually, reaching for a menu. "First I want to decide what to order."

"Where are Grace, Belinda, and Mandy?" Ellen asked.

"I told the traitors we weren't meeting until three-thirty because I don't think they're going to be cooperative." Janet set down her menu. "I think I'll have a Casey's Special."

"How can you eat at a time like this?" Lila

said dramatically. "Let alone four scoops of ice cream on a brownie!"

"Don't forget the whipped cream and cherry," Janet reminded Lila. She reached for her backpack and took out Winston's folded petition. "Is this what you're all so worked up about?"

"Of course!" Jessica said impatiently.

"Maybe you should take a closer look at it, Jess," Janet said with a mysterious smile.

"I already know what it says," Jessica snapped. "I don't need to see it."

"Oh, but you *do*," Janet urged, holding the petition up in the air. Suddenly she ripped it in two. "Here," she said casually, handing Jessica half of the paper, "take a look for yourself."

Jessica examined the torn page in her hand. Maybe Janet wasn't so dumb after all!

"Would you like to take a look, too, Tamara?" Janet continued. She ripped the half-page she was holding into two and handed a piece to Tamara.

Jessica giggled. "How about you, Lila?" she asked. "Want a piece?" She ripped her section and handed part to Lila. "After all, it's only fair that we all take a careful look at Winston's petition!"

"I want a piece, too!" Kimberly said, laughing.

Jessica and Janet both flung pieces of the petition into the air. "Catch!"

Before long, Winston's petition lay scattered

in dozens of pieces on the table. By the time Grace and the others arrived, the group was laughing uproariously.

"What's going on?" Grace asked, sliding into the booth next to Jessica. "It looks like it snowed in here."

When no one answered, she picked up a piece of paper and examined it closely. Suddenly her expression darkened. "You didn't! How could you destroy Winston's petition?"

"Easy," Lila explained. "You just take the paper and keep tearing."

"But this isn't fair!" Belinda protested.

"Look, Belinda," Janet said, "what Ms. Langberg doesn't know won't hurt us!"

"Watch out!" Ellen said in a low whisper, nodding toward the door.

Elizabeth, Amy, Ken, and Todd had just entered. When Elizabeth caught sight of Jessica, she waved and smiled.

"Let's hide the evidence," Jessica suggested, "or I'll never hear the end of it!"

As they swept up the little bits of paper, Jessica felt an annoying twinge of guilt. Elizabeth would not approve of what they had done. But then, Elizabeth wasn't a Booster, was she? Taking Winston's side was easy for her. She didn't have anything at stake.

Jessica had a handful of paper in her hand

when Elizabeth arrived at the Unicorns' booth. "Hi, Lizzie," she said as she dropped her hand under the table and let the paper flutter to the floor.

Elizabeth looked around. "What's going on?" she asked suspiciously.

"It can't be a Boosters meeting," Amy said. "Otherwise I would have been notified, right?"

"Of course we would have let you know," Janet said, speaking up quickly. "This is a Unicorn meeting."

"What's all that paper on the floor?" Ken asked, pointing at the ground. "It looks like there was a blizzard in here."

"That was my math quiz," Jessica said loudly. "I, um, got a D on it, and I was so annoyed that I tore it up into a million tiny pieces." She nudged Lila in the side. "Right, Lila?"

"Right," Lila said with conviction. "A big, fat D."

Elizabeth tapped her finger on her chin. "Dad and Mom sure will be sorry to hear about this, Jess," she said.

"There's no need to tell Mom and Dad," Jessica wheedled. "It was just a little quiz, not a major test or anything."

Todd bent down and picked up a piece of the paper. "Hey, look!" he said. "This isn't a math quiz! It's part of Winston's petition!"

"Really?" Jessica said, shrinking into her seat. "Gee, I must have torn it up by mistake."

Elizabeth looked disappointed. "Jessica! How could you do this?"

"It wasn't just Jessica," Janet finally said. "It was all of us. And it's none of your business, anyway, Elizabeth. You're not a Booster."

"She may not be, but *I* am!" Amy shouted. "This time you guys have gone too far!" She looked at Grace. "How could you let them do this?"

"I wasn't here," Grace replied, her eyes dark with anger. "I'm as mad as you are!"

"Look, this is totally unfair," Elizabeth said angrily. "You can't discriminate against Winston just because he's a guy. Winston has as much right to be a Booster as the rest of you."

Todd nodded toward the door. "There's Winston now," he whispered. "You don't want him to hear all this, do you?"

"He might as well," Amy said. "It's his petition."

Winston entered the crowded ice cream parlor with Randy and Leslie. When he saw Elizabeth, he waved.

"Looks like half the sixth grade is here," Winston said as he approached. His face darkened when he noticed Elizabeth's frown. "Is something wrong?"

Elizabeth pointed toward the floor.

Winston followed her gaze. When he saw the pile of paper, his face remained expressionless. "Let me guess," he said calmly, looking straight at Janet. "My petition, right?"

"Sorry," Janet said. "Better luck next time."

"Maybe you could start another petition," Todd suggested.

"Of course, the same kind of unfortunate accident might happen again," Janet pointed out.

"They have no right to do this, Winston!" Elizabeth said.

"That's OK, Elizabeth," Winston said, shrugging. "I can take care of myself. Besides, they don't have me beat yet."

Winston walked away, with Randy and Leslie close behind.

"What did he mean by that?" Jessica wondered aloud.

Janet shrugged. "Search me." She glanced around the room, an annoyed expression on her face. "*Where* is our waitress? I'm going to die of hunger if I don't get my Casey's Special right away."

"Come on, everybody," Elizabeth said. "Let's go somewhere else to eat. Suddenly I've lost my appetite for ice cream."

"Elizabeth?" Jessica called as her twin walked

away. "Do me a favor and don't bring up the math quiz, OK?"

"You mean that story was true?"

"Not the part about tearing it up. Just the part about the D," Jessica admitted.

Elizabeth settled next to Amy at a table in the mall's food court. "I still can't believe the way the Boosters are treating Winston."

Amy offered the bag of chocolate chip cookies she had just bought to Elizabeth, Ken, and Todd. "I can believe it," she said. "It's exactly their style."

"Personally, I think you're both making too big a deal out of this," Ken said as he reached for a cookie. "I mean, Winston can't be that serious about becoming a Booster."

"Why would he put up with all this abuse if he weren't serious?" Elizabeth asked. "I wish there were some way to get through to Jessica and the others."

Todd tapped his fingers on the table. "You know, Winston *did* say he can take care of himself."

"I know," Elizabeth replied. "But I still wish I could help him somehow."

"You've been talking about him for the last half-hour," Todd said irritably.

Elizabeth smiled. "Remember that time I told Winston to pay more attention in English class? *You* were the one who stood up for him then, Todd!"

"That was a whole different story," Todd insisted. "When you were bossing him around like that, you insulted his intelligence."

"So first you don't like it when I boss Winston around," Elizabeth teased, "and now you don't like it when I support him!"

Ken laughed. "Elizabeth is Winston's very own private cheerleader, Todd," he joked, punching Todd in the shoulder.

Todd glared at Ken. For a moment, nobody at the table said a word.

Finally Amy spoke. "Aren't these cookies amazing?" she asked. "I could eat a hundred of them."

"I'm getting a soda," Todd said, shoving back his chair abruptly.

Elizabeth watched as he walked away. She knew Todd was upset with her. Could it be he was actually jealous of her friendship with Winston? She pushed the thought out of her mind. Todd, jealous? Impossible.

Thursday morning Jessica was standing by her locker talking with Janet and Lila when Ms. Langberg suddenly appeared.

"Girls, I'd like to speak with you," she said sternly.

"But the first bell just rang," Janet protested lamely.

"In my office. Now," Ms. Langberg said.

The three girls trailed behind Ms. Langberg.

"What do you think this is about?" Jessica whispered to Lila.

Ms. Langberg whipped around. "You'll know soon enough."

"Good ears," Jessica whispered even more softly.

"You'd better believe it," Ms. Langberg said loudly.

They passed the gym and entered Ms. Langberg's tiny office. Trophies were piled on a file cabinet and three basketballs lay in the corner.

Ms. Langberg settled behind her desk. "I won't mince words, ladies, since it's almost time for homeroom," she said. "Give Winston an audition."

"Winston who?" Janet asked innocently.

"How many Winstons do you know, Janet?" Ms. Langberg asked sharply. "I'm referring to the one who put together a very impressive petition."

Janet smiled confidently. "There is no petition."

"Oh, really?" Ms. Langberg pulled open her

desk drawer and retrieved a sheet of paper. "Look familiar?" She passed the paper to Janet.

"It's Winston's petition!" Janet cried, her eyes wide with disbelief.

"It can't be!" Jessica blurted. "Yesterday we—"

"You *what*?" Ms. Langberg asked.

Jessica hung her head meekly. She knew when to keep her mouth shut, and this was definitely one of those moments.

"Does the word *photocopy* mean anything to you, Janet?" Lila snapped.

Ms. Langberg smiled slightly. "I recognize that this is difficult for you girls, but I want you to give Winston a fair and impartial tryout. If he's not up to the task, then at least you'll have given him a fair shot. And if he is—"

"Then the Boosters will be finished," Jessica said sadly.

Six

◇

"I still can't believe the Unicorns agreed to let Winston try out," Elizabeth said as she and Amy walked home from school on Friday afternoon. "I've never seen him so excited."

"He should be thanking Ms. Langberg," Amy said.

When they reached the Wakefields', Amy and Elizabeth headed into the den, where they found Jessica, Janet, Lila, Ellen, and Grace watching TV.

"Hi, Lizzie," Jessica called. She held up a plate of oatmeal cookies. "Look what Mom made us!"

Amy and Elizabeth sat down on the couch next to Ellen. "What are you watching?" Amy asked.

"It's a tape we borrowed from Ms. Langberg of last year's national cheerleading competition," Lila explained. "We're taking notes for Winston's tryout."

"What do you mean?" asked Grace, who was sitting on the floor near the TV. "I thought we were looking for new moves we could use for the cheerleading competition."

Janet waved her hand. "Well, that, too." She glanced at Jessica. "But mostly we wanted to think up some impossible stuff to make Winston do."

"I don't know why we're bothering," Ellen said. "That dweeb probably couldn't do a somersault to save his life!"

"Don't you ever give up?" Amy said. "Why can't you let him try out fair and square?"

"You are the most *un*loyal cheerleader," Ellen exclaimed.

Jessica reached for the remote control and clicked off the tape. "I almost forgot! There's this great made-for-TV movie on. Shelby Lane is in it. You know—the girl on *Days of Turmoil* who has amnesia?"

"Jessica! Turn it back to the cheerleading," Janet commanded. "This is more important than some movie. Besides, I've already seen it."

"Well, *I* haven't, and Shelby's one of my all-time favorite actresses," Jessica retorted. "Besides, if I'm ever going to be a soap opera star—"

"Since when are you going to be a soap opera star?" Elizabeth asked.

"I've always wanted to be an actress, Elizabeth. It's in my blood."

Janet grabbed the remote control away from Jessica. "Then try out for the drama club," she snapped. "But cheerleading is in *my* blood, and right now I say we watch the championship."

Elizabeth stood up. "Come on, Amy," she said. As she passed by Jessica, Elizabeth grabbed the plate of cookies.

"Hey!" Jessica cried, but it was too late. Elizabeth was already halfway to the kitchen.

A few minutes later Amy and Elizabeth were sitting at the kitchen table when Grace appeared in the doorway. "Mind if I join you?" she asked.

"Have a seat," Elizabeth offered. "And a cookie."

Grace reached for a cookie and nibbled on it thoughtfully. "I agree with both of you that the Boosters are being unfair to Winston. And to tell you the truth, I think it would be kind of fun to have a guy on the Boosters. Especially Winston." She looked over at Amy with an embarrassed smile. "I mean, he's so *nice* and everything."

"It doesn't look like there's much chance he'll get on the squad now," Amy said, sighing. "Not with the kind of tryout they're planning. It reminds me of my tryout for the squad, remember? The bleachers were packed with people, and it was my turn to do a cheer. Jessica, Ellen, Lila, and Janet stood next to me, promising to do the cheer with me so I wouldn't be all alone. Then, just as I yelled 'Ken, Ken, he's our man!' at the top of my lungs, they all ran off, leaving me there to cheer all by myself. I thought I'd die of embarrassment."

"But you didn't," Elizabeth reminded her. "You went right ahead with the cheer, and then you amazed everyone with your baton routine."

"Who knows?" Grace said. "Maybe Winston can do the same thing."

Elizabeth shook her head. "I don't know, Grace. He told me he took some gymnastics lessons this summer. But I have the feeling that nothing could prepare him for the audition the Boosters are planning." Suddenly an idea hit her. "You guys feel like taking a walk?" she asked. "I think we should pay a visit to Winston. The least we can do is warn him about the tryout."

Amy looked at Grace. "Janet will kill us if she finds out."

Grace shrugged. "Then we won't let her find out, will we?"

Winston stood on the wide lawn in back of his house and tried to pretend he was in the gymnasium at school. He closed his eyes, imagining the bleachers full of students. He could almost hear the gym exploding with their thunderous applause. He could see the Boosters watching him in amazement as he dazzled them with his talent.

When he opened his eyes he was back in his own yard. His little sister's swing set stood where the Boosters had been. His cat, Fuzzball, was his only audience.

Come on, Winston, he told himself, *you can do it!* He moved to the corner of the yard and did a string of perfect cartwheels across the lawn. He paused for breath, and looked at his audience. Fuzzball rolled over on her back and yawned.

For the hundredth time that day, Winston wondered if he was crazy to pursue this tryout. Chances were, no matter how good he was at his audition, the Boosters would find some excuse to keep him out. And what if he wasn't any good? What if he completely embarrassed himself?

"Are we interrupting anything?"

Winston spun around to see Elizabeth, Amy, and Grace approaching. "N-no," he stammered in surprise.

"We saw your cartwheels from down the block," Amy said brightly. "They looked great."

"Fuzzball didn't think so," Winston said, pointing to his cat. "She slept through most of it."

Grace walked over and stroked the dozing cat. "She's awfully pretty," she said, "even if she *doesn't* have any school spirit."

Winston smiled at Grace. *She's the prettiest girl in school*, he thought.

"So, how's the practicing coming?" Amy asked as she settled onto one of the swings.

Winston shrugged. "OK, I guess."

For a moment the girls were silent. Winston cleared his throat uncomfortably. He was probably supposed to do something polite, such as invite them in for cookies and milk. The trouble was, he wasn't sure there *were* any cookies inside. His mother had just left for the grocery store.

"Would you like to come in for something to eat?" he asked. "I'm pretty sure we have some stale graham crackers. And water—I know we have water!"

The three girls exchanged glances. "Winston," Elizabeth began, "the reason we came by is, um, we thought there was something you should know before you go any further with the Boosters tryout."

Winston saw worry in the three girls' faces. "What is it?" he asked.

"The Boosters are planning to make your audition really tough. They want to embarrass you in front of the whole school." Elizabeth looked him straight in the eye. "We were wondering if maybe you should . . ."

"Give up?" Winston said, finishing Elizabeth's sentence.

"You don't know the Boosters, Winston," Grace put in. "They can make things really hard on you."

"Not *all* the Boosters are that way," Winston said firmly. "How about you and Amy?"

"We'll stick up for you, but we're outnumbered," Grace said.

Winston smiled. It was nice to know he had someone on his side. "What's the worst that can happen? If I make a fool of myself, it won't be the first time. And it probably won't be the last!" he said.

"It's just that we don't want them to embarrass you, Winston," Amy continued.

"Look, there are lots of things worse than embarrassment," Winston said. "There's not even trying, for one. After all, you didn't have much of a chance with the Boosters, either, Amy, and look what you did!"

"He's right, you guys," Grace said firmly. "And you know what? I think it's going to work. The Boosters are going to be coed whether they like it or not!"

Winston looked at her gratefully. Inside, he still felt like a bundle of nerves, but how could he fail with people like Grace on his side?

"Well, thanks for the graham crackers, Winston," Elizabeth said as he walked the girls out into his front yard a half-hour later.

"Thank you for coming by. At least I'll know that when I try out, three people will be cheering for me."

Just then Elizabeth spotted Todd riding down the street on his bicycle. "Todd!" she called happily, waving. But instead of stopping, Todd coasted right on by, staring straight ahead.

"That was strange," Amy said as they watched Todd pedal hard and whip around the corner.

"Maybe he didn't hear me," Elizabeth said, but she was almost certain he had.

Once again the uneasy suspicion that Todd was growing jealous of Winston began to gnaw at her. How was she ever going to convince Todd that Winston was just a friend?

Seven

◇

"What's wrong, Elizabeth?" Jessica asked that evening before dinner. "You seem awfully quiet. You're not still mad about Winston's tryout, are you? After all, it's really Booster business."

"I still think you're being unfair to him," Elizabeth said as she placed silverware on the table. "But I don't feel like fighting about it."

"Why are you always defending Winston?" Jessica shot back. "You act as if the Boosters don't have rights, too."

"I am *not* always defending Winston," Elizabeth growled. Was that what Todd thought, too?

"What about Winston?" asked Steven, the twins' fourteen-year-old brother, as he strode into the kitchen. He headed straight for the pot of spaghetti sauce, lifted the lid, and took a swipe at it with a piece of bread. "Mmm," he said.

"Winston is Elizabeth's new boyfriend," Jessica said with an exaggerated grin.

"What happened to Todd?" Steven asked.

"*Nothing* happened to Todd," Elizabeth said irritably. "At least, I hope not."

Jessica leaned forward. "Did you and Todd have a fight over Winston Egbert?" she asked. She shook her head wisely. "I knew this would catch up with you, Elizabeth. Todd's obviously jealous of all the attention you're paying to Winston."

Just then Mr. and Mrs. Wakefield walked in. "Dinner will be ready in about fifteen minutes," Mrs. Wakefield said. "I just want to finish up some plans for the new office my firm is decorating." She glanced over at Elizabeth. "Is something wrong, honey?"

"Guy trouble," Jessica answered.

"What kind of guy trouble?" Mr. Wakefield asked.

"Too many guys, from the sound of it," Steven teased.

"I do *not* have too many guys. Why can't anyone believe that Winston and I are just friends?"

"*We* believe you, Lizzie," Jessica said, but her smile said otherwise. "The problem is Todd. Does *he* believe you?"

*   *   *

"Look at this crowd!" Jessica scanned the gym. "The bleachers are practically full!"

"Everyone wants to watch Winston fall on his face," Janet remarked.

All weekend Jessica and the Boosters had talked about Winston's tryout. By the time Monday afternoon came around, they were completely prepared. There was no way Winston could survive the audition they had planned.

The Boosters lined up in front of the crowd, Jessica basking in all the attention. She smiled up at the stands, knowing she looked great in her new uniform.

"Sexist pigs!" shouted a loud male voice. Several people laughed. A few even applauded.

Jessica glared furiously at the crowd above her. "We are *not* sexists," she protested. "How dare that creep call us that!"

"Who cares about the sexist part?" Lila demanded, thrusting her chin into the air. "We're not *pigs*!"

Janet leaned over. "There's Ms. Langberg," she whispered. "Remember! Be nice to Winston, no matter how hard it is."

"Where is our little cheerleader, anyway?" Lila asked. "Do you think he's chickening out?"

At that moment Winston trotted out onto the gym floor.

"Win-*ston*! Win-*ston*!" a small group chanted,

while the rest of the audience burst into a noise that seemed to be half cheering, half booing.

Winston ran across the gym and stood in front of the Boosters. He was wearing black sweatpants, a black T-shirt, and what looked like brand-new sneakers.

"Nice outfit, Winston," Ellen commented. "Did somebody die?"

"Ellen!" Janet snapped. She stood next to Winston and gave him a forced smile. "I think you look great, Winston," she said.

Ms. Langberg walked over. "Hello, Winston," she said, clapping him on the back. "I see you've attracted quite a crowd."

"It's my fan club," he said, glancing up at the sea of faces in the bleachers. "Well," he added, "some of them are, anyway."

"Let's get this show on the road, Janet," Ms. Langberg said.

"I thought we'd start out with some simple stuff to let Winston get warmed up first," Janet said sincerely. She looked at Ms. Langberg and smiled sweetly.

"Fine," Ms. Langberg replied. "Just get on with it." She headed for the bleachers and sat down.

Janet signaled for the rest of the Boosters to line up next to her. Then she directed Winston to the middle of the line, next to Jessica.

"OK, everybody," she said, "Winston Egbert has decided he would like to try out for the Boosters. We're going to start with a little warmup cheer to get everybody into the spirit of things." Janet turned and whispered to the group, "Let's start with 'Lean to the Left,' OK?"

Janet hadn't bothered to ask Winston if he knew the routine, Jessica noticed. She sneaked a peek at him out of the corner of her eye. There was a thin layer of perspiration on his upper lip, and she was almost certain that his hands were trembling. For a brief moment, an unexpected wave of admiration washed over Jessica. She wouldn't have the guts to do what Winston was doing.

Janet stepped forward and began the cheer. "Lean to the left! Lean to the right!" the girls shouted.

As the Boosters chanted, Jessica was surprised to hear Winston's deeper voice blending with their own. She glanced over and was shocked to see him moving in perfect unison with the group, his arms swinging energetically, his steps precise.

"Stand up! Sit down! Fight! Fight! Fight!" the Boosters cried. Janet began to repeat the cheer and then stepped aside so she could watch Winston more carefully. The crowd began to cheer along, swaying from side to side.

Jessica could tell by Janet's grim expression that she was as surprised as Jessica was by Winston's performance.

When the cheer was done, Janet stepped back over to the group. "Not bad," she told Winston, "for a beginner."

"Thanks," he said breathlessly.

"Let's try some solo work now," Janet said. She winked at Jessica. "How about the 'He's Our Man!' cheer?" she asked casually, as if the idea had just occurred to her.

Jessica nodded and stepped forward. They had planned on this cheer, hoping it would embarrass Winston when they forced him to cheer for another guy.

The other Boosters sat down, and Jessica stood before the crowd, hands on hips. "Bruce! Bruce! He's our man! If he can't do it, no one can!" She finished with a graceful, high leap, and the crowd roared its approval. As she passed by Winston she could tell he was shaken.

"Your turn, Winston," Janet instructed loudly. "Try to show as much spirit as Jessica— even if you *are* cheering for another guy."

Winston stepped to the middle of the gym, hands on hips. "I think I'll update this cheer a little, if you don't mind," he said, smiling at the Boosters' bench. "After all, we have to remember the girls' teams, too."

Before anyone could answer, he began to chant. "Grace! Grace!" he yelled, loud and clear. "Give her a hand! If she can't do it, no one can!" He finished the cheer with a perfect leap, higher than any of the Boosters had ever seen, let alone done.

"That was wonderful!" Grace cheered as the audience burst into loud applause.

As she scanned the stands, Jessica was surprised to see Todd, Aaron Dallas, and Ken clapping appreciatively along with the rest of the crowd. *Don't they realize how ridiculous it looks to have a guy cheering with a bunch of girls?* she wondered.

Janet headed for the center of the gym. "Enough of the easy stuff," she said. "Now we're going to get down to business!"

She motioned for the Boosters to set up a series of mats on the floor. "Jessica and I will act as spotters," she told Winston. "We're going to have you try some simple gymnastics stunts. Nothing we can't do in our sleep, but if you can't handle it, just say the word."

Winston nodded nervously.

"Let's start with some simple somersaults," Janet instructed.

Winston obeyed, rolling across the mats effortlessly.

Janet looked over at Jessica. "How about some cartwheels?" she asked.

"Two-handed or one-handed?" Winston asked, brushing off his knees as he stood at the end of the last mat.

"No-handed!" Jessica answered, winking at Janet. That would end the charade quickly, she figured. No-handed cartwheels were very difficult.

Winston rubbed his hands together and swallowed hard. He looked up into the audience at Elizabeth, who waved. Then he took a deep breath and flew across the mat, his legs drawing perfect circles in the air.

Jessica stared openmouthed at Winston as he waved to the cheering crowd. This was impossible! It was almost as bad as Amy's tryout, when she had surprised everyone with her baton skills. Jessica ran over to Janet to consult while Winston waited by the mats, flushed with exertion.

"*Now* what?" Janet moaned. "He was supposed to be flat on his face by now."

The Boosters huddled together, with the exception of Amy and Grace, who were obviously enjoying the show. "How about handsprings?" Ellen offered.

"Or make him stand on his head," Tamara said. "No one can do that in front of a huge crowd like this!"

Jessica and Janet headed back to the mats. "We'll need to see some *very* professional handsprings," Janet told him.

Winston grinned confidently. "Front or back?"

Janet looked as if she might explode. "Whatever," she said, waving her hand dismissively.

"How about both?" Winston asked. He took a deep breath and did a series of perfect back handsprings in one direction and front handsprings in the other, popping off the mats with breathtaking energy.

Again the crowd roared its approval. Jessica looked over at Ms. Langberg, who was shaking her head in amazement.

"One more thing," Jessica said suddenly. "It's a requirement that all Boosters be able to do a headstand for a full thirty seconds."

"I don't remember that requirement," Ms. Langberg called.

"That's OK, Ms. Langberg," Winston assured her. "I love headstands."

"It figures," Jessica said under her breath.

Winston marched to the middle of a mat and bent down, carefully placing his hands and head in a triangle before slowly raising up his legs until he was perfectly vertical. Somebody in the stands began counting backward as the seconds ticked by on the big gymnasium clock.

Soon the whole gym was chanting along. "Twenty-six, twenty-five, twenty-four . . ."

"Now what?" Jessica demanded, rushing over to Janet.

Janet hung her head. "We've run out of stuff. Face it, Jess, he's a better gymnast than the rest of us put together!"

When the countdown was done, the crowd burst into wild applause. Winston waved triumphantly and ran over to the bench where the Boosters were sitting. Jessica watched as he whispered something to Grace, and the two of them walked over to the mats.

Winston bent down and Grace stepped carefully onto his shoulders, balancing with her arms while he held her ankles and slowly stood. The room grew perfectly still. Suddenly Grace seemed to fly through the air, executing a perfect somersault while the crowd gasped in awe. She landed on her feet and smiled widely.

The audience stood and applauded so loudly the entire room seemed to shake. Jessica looked over at Ms. Langberg and felt her heart sink to her knees. The P.E. teacher was standing, too, applauding and grinning broadly.

"It's all over," she whispered to Janet. "The Boosters will never be the same again."

Eight

◇

" 'Victory for Winston Egbert!' " Elizabeth said, reading the headline of the *Sixers* article she had written the previous night.

It was Tuesday morning, and the whole school was still buzzing with talk of Winston's remarkable performance. Elizabeth had written a special front-page story about it for the *Sixers*. She was standing next to her locker showing the hand-written article to Grace and Amy when Winston passed by.

"Winston! Take a look at this!" Elizabeth called. "You're about to become famous!"

Winston looked at the headline and gave a low whistle. "Wow," he said, "I feel like a real superstar. Now all I need is some groupies," he added.

"Hey," Amy said, "I've been dying to ask you and Grace something. How did you two manage to pull off that stunt at the end of your tryout yesterday? Had you ever done anything like that before?"

"I did a lot of that in gymnastics class last summer," Winston explained. He smiled at Grace. "And I was sure Grace could pull it off without a hitch."

"Weren't you nervous, Grace?" Elizabeth asked.

"A little," Grace admitted. "But after watching Winston try out, I had total faith in him."

"You know, if we can add some stunts like that to our regular Boosters routine, we'll have a much better shot at the championship," Amy said excitedly. "I can't wait till practice this afternoon!"

"Me, too!" Grace agreed.

"Me, three!" Winston said with a laugh as he headed off down the hall.

He couldn't remember when he had felt so great. He'd overcome his shyness, his self-doubt, and, of course, the opposition of the Boosters. And by sticking to his goal, he had been able to accomplish something amazing—something no other guy in the school had the nerve to do. And to top it all off, he had become sort of a celebrity.

Winston smiled to himself as he turned the corner. People seemed to be looking at him in a whole new way.

Suddenly Winston noticed several students gathered in front of his locker, laughing and pointing. Even from several feet away, he could see why.

Someone had covered his locker with flowery pink wrapping paper and three huge pink bows.

Bruce Patman, a seventh grader whom Winston had never liked, strode up, an obnoxious grin spread across his face. "Nice locker, *Winnie*," he sneered.

Winston took a deep breath and pressed through the crowd. He dropped his books and began tearing at the wrapping paper, crumpling pieces of it and tossing them to the ground angrily. But whoever had done the prank had done it carefully, using plenty of tape, and the awful decorations refused to come off without a fight.

"Let me give you a hand."

It was Elizabeth. She joined Winston and peeled off a bow with her fingernail.

"Thanks, Elizabeth," Winston said. He managed a short laugh. "It's funny," he mused. "Usually I *like* opening presents!"

Elizabeth smiled grimly. "What kind of jerk could have done this?"

Behind them came a giggle. They looked over

their shoulders and saw several of the Unicorns, including Jessica, watching from a distance.

"Jessica!" Elizabeth cried, whirling around. "Did you have anything to do with this stupid prank?"

"Me?" Jessica said innocently. "You know I can't tie a decent bow, Elizabeth! I always make *you* wrap all my Christmas presents!"

"Hey, Winston," Lila called. "Save the bows. They'll look *darling* in your hair!"

The Unicorns dashed off. Elizabeth started to follow them, but Winston grabbed her arm to stop her. "It's just a joke, Elizabeth," he said. "I'm going to have to take a little teasing until people get used to the idea of a male cheerleader."

Elizabeth set off down the hall to her third-period class, still fuming over the Boosters' stupid trick. As she looked over to check the hallway clock, she caught sight of Todd in the crowd.

"Todd!" she called loudly, but he didn't seem to hear her in the noisy hallway traffic.

Elizabeth threaded her way through the crowd until she fell into step beside him. "Hi," she said breathlessly. "I called you, but I guess you couldn't hear me."

For a moment Todd didn't answer. "What were you doing with Winston?" he asked finally. "I saw you two together in the hall."

"I was just helping him clean off his locker," Elizabeth explained. "The Boosters played a nasty trick on him."

"I know," Todd said. She thought she saw a hint of a smile on his lips. "I saw."

Elizabeth felt her annoyance return. It wasn't like Todd to think a stupid stunt such as that was funny. She reached for his arm and pulled him toward the wall.

"You didn't think that locker prank was funny, did you?" Elizabeth asked.

Todd looked away, refusing to meet Elizabeth's eyes. "You know how I feel about the Unicorns," he said. "But it was just a harmless joke, Elizabeth. And anyway, Winston's a big boy. I'm sure you know all *about* Winston, though. You two have spent enough time together lately."

"Todd," Elizabeth said, searching his face, "don't you understand that Winston and I are just good friends?"

"You're friends with lots of guys," Todd replied. "But you don't spend *all* your time with them."

Elizabeth stared at Todd. How could she get through to him? "Winston's been having a tough time lately, Todd. He needs a friend right now."

Todd stared at Elizabeth and swallowed hard. "I've got to go, Elizabeth," he said. "I'm already late for class."

Elizabeth watched Todd race off down the

now-deserted hall. She called his name, but he had already turned the corner and disappeared.

By lunchtime, Winston had nearly forgotten the locker incident. So many students—girls *and* guys—had congratulated him on his performance the previous day that the Boosters' prank had faded from his mind.

He had just finished buying his lunch and was walking through the cafeteria when he noticed Charlie Cashman standing on top of a chair. Charlie, a sixth grader, had a reputation for being a bully, and Winston instantly sensed he was up to something.

"Give me a *W*!" Charlie shouted, cupping his hands around his mouth. He looked straight at Winston as he continued, "Give me an *I*!"

A few of Charlie's friends joined in. "*I*!" they yelled.

Winston headed for an empty seat next to Randy Mason. "Give me an *N*! Give me another *N*!" Charlie continued.

Winston set down his tray. "Why do I have the feeling that I know what this is going to spell?" he said.

"Give me an *I*! Give me an *E*!" Charlie screamed gleefully. "What does it spell?"

Winston stood perfectly still, waiting for the response.

"Winnie!" Charlie yelled.

"Winnie! Winnie!" his friends screamed in a raucous chorus.

Briefly Winston considered crawling under the lunch table. He glanced over at the Unicorner. He could tell that Janet and most of the others were thrilled by Charlie's little cheer. Taking a deep breath, Winston turned toward Charlie and began to applaud. Charlie stopped yelling, obviously confused.

"Great job, Charlie," Winston called. "Keep up the good work and we'll make a place on the squad for *you!*"

To his relief, the lunchroom exploded in laughter. Charlie looked around, visibly embarrassed. After a moment, he climbed down off his chair.

"Good one, Winston," Randy Mason said as Winston took his seat.

"Way to go, Winston!" someone else yelled.

Winston sighed with relief and looked over at the Unicorner again. Grace and Mandy smiled and waved. The others looked thoroughly disappointed.

Winston reached for his hamburger and took a bite. To his delight, it was still warm. It was hard to remember when a lunchroom hamburger had ever tasted so good.

* * *

Winston was on his way to the gym after school when he remembered the list of cheers he had compiled the night before. Turning around, he dashed back to his locker.

The hall was deserted, and his footsteps echoed loudly. He opened his locker and rifled through a notebook until he found the sheet of paper he needed.

Suddenly Winston had the uneasy feeling he wasn't alone. Slowly he turned, and what he saw made him gulp with fear.

There stood Charlie Cashman, flanked by two huge eighth-grade boys. "Nobody makes fun of me and gets away with it," Charlie sneered as he moved in closer. "*Especially* not you, Winnie!"

Winston stood his ground, although his heart seemed to be caught in his throat. "Come on, Charlie," he croaked. "It was all in good fun."

Charlie and the two big bullies took another step closer. "Where are you going, Winnie, to your ballet lesson?" Charlie asked, chuckling.

Winston clenched his fists. It was three against one, and he didn't have a prayer with those odds—especially when two of the three were eighth-grade gorillas. He took a step forward. "OK, guys," he said, trying to talk around the lump in his throat, "it's been swell talking with you, but—"

"Not so fast," Charlie said, thrusting Winston

back against his locker with a thud. "We're not quite through with *her*, are we, guys?"

One of the boys grabbed hold of Winston's right arm, while the other pinned his left arm to the wall. Winston watched in horror as Charlie's fist came at him. The impact at the corner of his eye knocked his head hard against the locker. It had all happened so quickly.

Charlie smiled triumphantly. "See you around, Winnie," he said as his two friends released Winston. As they started to leave, Charlie added, "Don't worry about that shiner, Winnie. A little eye makeup should cover it up just fine!"

As Winston watched the boys stride off, he touched his finger to his eye. It was throbbing, and he knew it would be black and blue before long. He didn't know which hurt more—his eye or his pride.

Nine

◇

The Boosters were gathered in the girls' locker room Tuesday after school. Janet peeked around a wall of lockers. "Has anyone seen Grace or Amy?"

When no one answered, Janet pointed to Jessica. "You're in charge of Winston's sabotage. Take over."

"Yes, sir!" Jessica said, giving Janet a mock salute. She pulled a piece of paper and a pencil out of her gym bag. "Let's go down the checklist and make sure we're prepared," she said, savoring her moment of power. She had been on the phone for hours the night before, preparing for the sabotage campaign. So far, things had been going very well. She was particularly proud of the decorations on Winston's locker, since that had been her idea. Charlie Cashman's cheer at lunch hadn't been planned, though everyone agreed it had helped. And that afternoon's round of pranks would be the most important of all.

"You all know the signal, right?" Jessica asked. "I pull on my right earlobe." She demonstrated for the group. "Let's see now." She consulted her list. "Lila, peanut butter."

Lila pulled a jar of extra-chunky peanut butter out of her gym bag. "Check," she said. "I even brought a spoon."

"Ellen," Jessica continued. "Quick-dry glue."

"Roger." Ellen nodded. "The tube says it dries in sixty seconds."

"Good work." Jessica checked Ellen and Lila off her list. "And last but not least, Kimberly."

Kimberly pointed to her jacket. "She's wrapped in there, sleeping like a baby."

"Looks like everything's all set," Jessica said. "Now you all know what you're supposed to—"

"Afternoon, ladies."

It was Ms. Langberg.

"I know I can count on you to make Winston feel welcome today," Ms. Langberg said, spinning the rope of her whistle around her index finger as she spoke. "This is going to be a big adjustment for you, but I think Winston will make a fine addition to the squad."

She turned and smiled as Grace and Amy

arrived. "Now, don't forget that the championship is less than two weeks away. I'm sure you'll be pleased to hear that I've ordered a uniform for Winston that should arrive in a few days."

Jessica raised her hand.

"Yes, Jessica?"

"Winston's uniform won't clash with ours, will it?" Jessica asked. "I mean, if it's not just the right shade of, uh, blue, we'll never live it down."

"Why don't you worry a little more about cheering and a little less about color-coordinating your uniforms?" Ms. Langberg suggested dryly. She paused, raising an eyebrow, and pointed to the jar of peanut butter in Lila's hand. "Hungry, Lila?" she asked.

Lila dropped the jar into her gym bag as if it were on fire. "I always say, be prepared," she answered.

"Right," Ms. Langberg said doubtfully.

The girls filed into the gym and began to stretch.

"Where *is* Winston, anyway?" Jessica asked. "He could at least be on time."

Another five minutes passed before the gym doors swung open and Winston appeared. He was wearing his sweatpants, and his sneakers were slung over his shoulder. "Sorry I'm late," he said. "I had an unfortunate, uh, run-in."

Jessica looked up from her leg stretches.

"Your eye!" she cried. "What did you do, run into a door?"

"No, actually, I ran into Charlie Cashman's fist." Winston dropped down onto a bleacher.

"Winston!" Grace cried, rushing over. "He *hit* you?"

"That rotten bully," Amy seethed. "Does it hurt much?"

"Only when I look in the mirror."

"Maybe you should go home and rest," Janet suggested hopefully.

"Sorry, Janet. You're not getting rid of me that easily."

"OK, line up, everybody!" Janet yelled, clapping her hands.

"Just a second, Janet," Winston said. "I need to change into my sneakers."

Jessica shot Janet an anxious look. "Don't worry about that yet, Winston," Jessica said airily. "We just need to decide where to place you in line."

"But shouldn't I have my gym shoes on?" Winston asked, reaching down to loosen his laces.

"Your regular shoes are just fine." Janet walked over and escorted Winston to the middle of the gym.

As she passed Lila, Jessica pulled on her right earlobe. Lila grabbed her gym bag and dashed over to the spot where Winston had left his sneakers.

"Now everybody line up, facing *away* from the bleachers," Janet instructed.

"Why?" Amy asked.

"Why what?" Janet responded, sounding annoyed.

"Why should we face away from the bleachers? Are you planning to have us cheer backward?"

Janet shot Amy a poisonous look. "*I* don't know why," she growled. "It was Ms. Langberg's idea. *She's* the P.E. professional, Amy."

Carefully Jessica sneaked a peek at Lila, who was skillfully scooping peanut butter into Winston's shoes.

"Let's see now," Janet mused, tapping her finger on her chin. "Winston's the tallest, so he'll have to go in the back row." She glanced over her shoulder at Lila, then turned back to the group, all smiles. "In fact, we might even create a whole new row for Winston. His very own row."

"Why?" Grace demanded in an accusing tone. "No one will be able to see him!"

"There's a point," Janet said.

Just then Lila raced up to join the group. "It's about time, Lila," Jessica snapped.

"OK, everybody, turn around," Janet instructed.

"Then why were we backward to begin with?" Grace demanded.

"Search me." Janet shrugged. "Go ask Ms. Langberg." Suddenly she stopped and stared down at Winston's feet. "Winston, you should know that you can't wear street shoes on the gym floor. Sneakers only!"

"I'll change, then," Winston said calmly.

Janet turned toward the rest of the Boosters, grinning wickedly. "Let's put some mats together," she commanded, glancing over her shoulder at Winston. "We'll start by practicing Jessica's pyramid."

"Oh, no!" Amy moaned.

"Anything but that!" Kimberly cried.

Winston came back to the lineup holding his shoes in the air. "Anybody hungry?" he said, a broad grin on his face. "Say, for some peanut butter on sole, maybe?" He returned his sneakers to the bleachers and dashed back over to the group in bare feet.

Jessica couldn't believe it. Winston didn't even seem fazed. In fact, he seemed to think the peanut butter in his sneakers was *funny*.

"You can't practice without shoes," Janet scolded.

"Then I'll just observe today," Winston said good-naturedly. "By the way, nice try with the shoes. Personally, Lila, I would have gone with creamy peanut butter instead of chunky."

"What are you talking about, Winston?" Amy asked.

"It's no big deal," he said, shrugging. "Now, about that pyramid—"

"Sorry, but there's no room for you in it, Winston," Jessica interrupted. He was already sabotaging her sabotage. She wasn't about to let him ruin her pyramid, too.

"I was going to say that maybe I could give you a few pointers."

"Good," Amy said emphatically. "We could use some!"

"The problem," Lila interjected, "is that Jessica insists on being on top, and we all agree she's way too heavy."

"I am not too heavy!" Jessica shot back, incensed. "You guys are just too pathetically weak."

"Let's not start *that* again," Janet moaned. "Jessica," she said meaningfully, "wasn't there something you had to do?"

Jessica, still fuming about Lila's remark, had nearly forgotten steps two and three of the sabotage plan. She pulled on her earlobe, and when that didn't work, she nudged Ellen.

Ellen's eyes lit up with sudden understanding

and she ran to the bleachers, where she had left her gym bag.

"The most important thing to remember about stunts involving balance is to have firm grounding," Winston began explaining.

Jessica glanced over at Kimberly and pulled hard on her earlobe. Unfortunately, Kimberly seemed to be fascinated by Winston's lecture.

Jessica cleared her throat. If she pulled any harder on her earlobe, it was going to be the size of a dinner plate.

To Jessica's relief, Tamara noticed her gesturing and gave Kimberly a swift kick in the shin.

"Ow!" Kimberly squeaked. Winston stopped speaking, and Kimberly glanced around furtively, looking embarrassed. "I mean, wow!" she said quickly. "You sure do know your pyramids, Winston!"

While he continued his lecture, Kimberly ran to the bleachers to retrieve her jacket. Wrapped inside was a rubber doll wearing a pink diaper. She hurried over to Winston's gym bag while Ellen completed her mission on the bleachers.

Jessica sighed with relief. So far, so good. But they didn't have much time now. The glue would be drying in a matter of seconds.

"Um, Winston?" she interrupted politely. "I have a great idea. Why don't we go ahead and do the pyramid while you watch from the bleachers?

That way you can tell us what we're doing wrong."

Winston nodded. "Sounds good to me." He strode over to the bleachers just as Ellen and Kimberly rejoined the group. Jessica held her breath. *Please sit in the same spot!* she pleaded silently.

To her relief, Winston settled right where he had been before, next to his gym bag—and right on top of the layer of clear glue that Ellen had just applied.

Jessica grinned at her coconspirators. As the bottom row of the pyramid lined up, Ellen and Lila began to giggle uncontrollably.

"What are you guys up to?" Amy demanded.

"*Us?*" Lila asked innocently.

"Now the first rule of pyramid-building," Winston instructed, "is: *Do not laugh*. One person starts to giggle, and before you know it, the whole pyramid will be wobbling like a bowl of Jell-O."

Instantly everybody began to giggle all the more.

"Now, who's on the bottom?" Winston asked, smiling.

"Lila, Kimberly, and me," Amy answered. "Unfortunately!"

"The important thing about you bottom people is to make sure that when you get down on all fours your hands and knees are evenly spaced,"

Winston said. "That way the weight will be distributed better."

"You mean *Jessica's* weight," Amy groaned.

After the first three girls were settled on the mat, Grace and Ellen climbed on top of them. "Same principle applies here," Winston instructed. "Balance carefully and distribute your weight." He watched for a moment, then said, "Now, for the big finale!"

"*Big* is the word, all right," Lila grumbled.

Jessica moved to kick Lila, but Winston interrupted.

"No kicking, Jessica!" he reminded her. "And no complaining, bottom row. I think you'll be surprised how light Jessica really is!"

Jessica smiled with satisfaction. Maybe Winston wasn't all bad.

"Now climb up carefully, Jessica. Think of yourself as a feather," Winston called.

"Yeah," Amy muttered. "A thousand-pound feather!"

Jessica climbed carefully onto Kimberly's back. From there, she hoisted herself up onto Grace and Ellen.

"Is she up yet?" Amy asked.

"Of course!" Winston responded.

"Amazing!" Amy marveled. "I can't even tell!"

"Told you so," Jessica said triumphantly as she raised herself to a standing position.

"Ladies and gentlemen," Winston cried, "may I present the new middle school cheering squad champions!"

Jessica leaped gracefully to the ground. "Thanks, Winston," she said. "I've been trying to tell these whiners what a great idea that was."

"You know, Tamara and Janet could continue the cheer on either side of the pyramid and do a big jump for the finale," Winston suggested eagerly. "And I could stand behind and be the spotter."

He started to get up, and suddenly Jessica remembered Ellen's glue. While the girls watched breathlessly, Winston kept trying to stand, but his sweatpants refused to budge. Finally he gave an extra-strong pull. The sound of ripping fabric echoed in the gym.

Winston took one look at his rear end and his face turned the color of a strawberry. Quickly he reached for his gym bag and pulled out his jacket to wrap around him.

"Well, I'll say one thing," he said, shaking his head. "You guys sure live up to your reputations!"

"Winston," Grace began, "we're not all responsible for this—"

"I know that, Grace," Winston said, tying his

jacket around his waist. "So, Janet, when's our next practice?"

"Tomorrow," Janet muttered.

"Until then," Winston said. He picked up his gym bag, and there, peeking out with a frozen smile, was Kimberly's doll.

Ten

◇

"I can't believe the Unicorns were so horrible to Winston this afternoon," Elizabeth said.

"All things considered, he held up pretty well," Amy said, shaking her head. The two girls were sitting in the Wakefields' den working on their homework. A large pile of science books from the library sat on the coffee table.

Jessica walked in and flopped onto the couch. "Whose turn is it to set the table tonight, Elizabeth?"

"Yours," Elizabeth snapped. "Jess, how could you have been so cruel to Winston today?"

"Winston, Winston, Winston," Jessica complained. "That's all I ever hear anymore."

"Isn't he your new male cheerleader?" Steven asked as he dropped into the big armchair near the TV.

Elizabeth nodded. "He won't be for long, if the Unicorns keep making his life miserable."

Jessica rolled onto her side. "You would have loved this, Steven! We glued Winston Egbert to a bleacher, and when he tried to get up, his sweatpants tore! It was hilarious!"

Steven, who loved practical jokes, was obviously impressed. "Not bad," he said, laughing appreciatively.

"Steven!" Elizabeth cried. "You're missing the whole point!"

"Lizzie has the hots for Winston," Jessica remarked.

"Hmm," Steven mused. "Elizabeth Egbert. It has a nice ring, don't you think, Jess?"

Elizabeth tossed a pillow at Steven.

Amy turned to Jessica. "At least admit this much, Jessica. Winston *did* improve your pyramid routine."

Jessica sat up abruptly. "For your information, Amy, that pyramid was fine before Winston Egbert ever showed up!" She stood and marched toward the kitchen.

"Hey, Jess?" Amy called. "How come your right earlobe's longer than your left one?"

Jessica spun around, grabbing her right ear. When Amy began to giggle, Jessica stomped out of the room.

"What was that about?" Elizabeth asked.

Amy shrugged. "Long story."

Steven looked over at Elizabeth. "So is this really serious?" he asked, grinning.

"Is *what* serious?"

"You and this Egbert guy."

Elizabeth took a deep breath. "Steven, would you mind disappearing? Amy and I have a lot of work to do on our science projects."

"Sure, sure," Steven said. "I can take a subtle hint." He headed for the kitchen.

"Want to buy a brother?" Elizabeth asked Amy. "I'll give you a real deal."

"He was just teasing, Elizabeth," Amy reminded her.

"I know," Elizabeth admitted. "It's just that—well, this whole Winston thing is getting out of hand. Why can't a girl and a guy just be friends without people jumping to the wrong conclusion? Even Todd is upset because I've been spending time with Winston." Elizabeth chewed on her lower lip. "I tried to explain it to him, but he wouldn't listen."

"It's only because he likes you so much," Amy assured her.

"I know that," Elizabeth replied. "I was even a little bit flattered at first." She sighed. "But now it's gone too far. I don't want to have to give up my friendship with Winston just so Todd can feel more secure."

"You're absolutely right. If the situation were reversed, I wonder how Todd would feel?"

Suddenly Elizabeth leaped off the couch. "Amy, that's it!" she said with a sly smile. "You and I are going to teach Todd Wilkins a lesson he'll never forget!"

"Boy, I don't feel like practicing today, do you?" Jessica asked Wednesday afternoon as she settled next to Grace on a bleacher.

"Sure," Grace said cheerfully as she scribbled away in the notebook she was holding in her lap. "I think we may have a fighting chance at the championship now that Winston is on our squad."

Jessica shrugged. "What are you drawing?"

"Nothing much," Grace said, snapping her notebook shut. "Just doodling."

"Everybody ready for a good workout?" Janet cried as she, Lila, and Tamara entered the gym.

"Janet," Jessica said, "how about we take today off? We're not going to have any spirit left for the competition at this rate. And besides, I've missed three days in a row of *Days of Turmoil!*"

Janet stopped in her tracks. "You don't really mean that a soap opera is more important to you than winning this championship, do you?"

Jessica sighed. She was getting tired of being pushed around by Janet. Putting up with her at Boosters practice once a week was bad enough, but having to deal with her every single day was more than any sane human being could handle.

She stood up, hands on her hips. "All I'm asking is that we take one lousy afternoon off, Janet. Everybody's tired. Our muscles hurt. And we're all behind on our homework." She added the last part as an afterthought for Amy.

"Jessica, I can't believe you," Janet shouted. "The championship is a week from Saturday, and you don't even care!"

"Of *course* I care!" Jessica shot back. "*You're* the one who—"

"Hi, everybody!"

Winston came dashing in and stepped between Jessica and Janet. Jessica noticed that his eye was now a startling shade of purple.

"What's the problem?" Winston asked.

"Jessica wants to call off practice today," Janet said, her arms crossed over her chest.

"I just think we could all use a day off," Jessica argued. As soon as the words were out of her mouth, she wondered why she was explaining this to Winston.

"Well," Winston said, "it's important that we practice as much as we can—"

"See?" Janet snapped at Jessica.

"But it's also important that we don't overdo it," Winston finished.

"See?" Jessica snapped back.

"Why don't we practice for half our normal time?" Winston said thoughtfully. "That way we still get some work done, and Jessica could get home in time for her soap."

"Sounds good to me," Janet said.

"Me, too," Jessica agreed. It seemed obvious when Winston put it that way. Then she cocked her head and eyed him carefully. "Wait a minute! How did you know I wanted to watch a soap?"

Winston shrugged. "Intuition."

Practice went smoothly after that. The squad attempted the pyramid formation, using all the members, and after a few tries they got the hang of it. It was still a bit wobbly, but even Jessica had to admit that the stunt was much more impressive, thanks to Winston's help.

The group was putting the finishing touches on a new cheer Winston had invented when Ken, Aaron, and Todd burst into the gym, pounding their basketballs loudly on the floor.

"We're supposed to have the gym for another half-hour," Janet informed the boys loudly.

Aaron tossed his ball through the basketball hoop and smiled at Jessica. She waved back, pleased to have the entire squad as witnesses.

"We just got here a little early," Ken said. "You mind if we watch?"

"Yes, actually," Janet replied. "You'll be too distracting."

"How's it going, Winston?" Todd asked.

"So far, so good," Winston replied.

Reluctantly, the boys began to leave. Just as they reached the door, Amy Sutton ran over to Todd.

"Amy!" Janet cried. "We're trying to work here!"

"Just one second," Amy replied. She said something to Todd, who nodded his head.

The boys left, and Amy ran back to her position. "I need some help with my science project," she explained nonchalantly. "And I asked Todd to help me."

"What kind of help?" Jessica asked. Amy was an excellent student. Why would she be asking Elizabeth's boyfriend for help?

"Science is Todd's favorite subject," Amy replied vaguely, avoiding Jessica's eyes. "And I could really use a good grade on my project."

"But why ask Todd?" Jessica pressed. Was there something fishy going on here? Jessica had excellent instincts about this kind of thing.

"Why not?" Amy responded. "It's a free country, Jessica. And I *like* Todd. Who doesn't? He's cute and nice—"

"But he's *Elizabeth's* boyfriend," Jessica interrupted.

"That doesn't mean he and I can't be friends," Amy replied.

"If you two don't stop chatting, we'll never get out of here early, and you'll miss your soap, Jess!" Janet scolded.

Jessica didn't care anymore. It looked like she might have her very own soap opera right under her nose!

Elizabeth was getting ready for bed that night when Jessica peeked into her bedroom. "Elizabeth?" she said. "Lizzie, I know you're kind of upset about this whole thing with Winston." She stepped into the room and sat on Elizabeth's bed. "I just want you to know that we're not planning any more pranks or anything." Jessica sighed. "I guess we all realize we're pretty much stuck with him."

Elizabeth sat next to Jessica on the bed. "I'm glad to hear that, Jess."

"I feel better," Jessica admitted. "I hated to have Winston come between the two of us." She paused for a moment, her expression dark.

"Is something wrong, Jess?"

Jessica examined her nails. "Lizzie, has Amy said anything to you about her science project?" she asked casually.

Elizabeth laughed. "What brought that up?"

"Oh, nothing, really," Jessica replied. "Well, has she?"

Elizabeth grinned. "She said she's a little worried about getting a good grade. And she mentioned something about frogs. Why?"

Jessica hopped off the bed. "No reason," she said. "I'm sure it was nothing."

"What was nothing?"

Jessica looked at Elizabeth. "Nothing. 'Night, Elizabeth."

Elizabeth waited until she heard Jessica's bedroom door close. Then she tiptoed out to the hallway phone and dialed Amy's number.

"Amy?" Elizabeth whispered. "Sorry to call so late."

"That's OK," Amy said. "I was just working out a diet for my frogs. Do you think they'd like pepperoni?"

"I doubt it," Elizabeth said, giggling. "I just wanted to tell you that you're doing a great job with our Todd plan. Jessica's already worried!"

"Poor Todd," Amy said. "I think he was a little surprised that I suddenly needed a science tutor!"

"Well, keep up the good work," Elizabeth said softly. "I'll see you tomorrow."

Elizabeth set the receiver down and smiled. Her plan was right on schedule.

Eleven

◇

"Elizabeth? Can I come in?" Grace asked shyly.

Elizabeth looked up from the article she was proofreading in the *Sixers* office. It was Friday morning, and she had arrived at school early to work on the paper.

"Sure, Grace," Elizabeth said with a smile. "I could use a little company."

Grace sat down across from Elizabeth in the cramped office. "I wanted to talk to you about the *Sixers*." She reached into her backpack and pulled out a notebook. "I had an idea." She paused, looking embarrassed. "You've probably got plenty of stuff for the next issue, though."

"We can always use a good story."

"It's not a story. It's a picture—lots of pictures, really." Grace flipped through her notebook nervously. "The thing is, I've been feeling really bad about the way the Boosters treated Winston."

"Me, too," Elizabeth agreed.

"So I thought maybe it would be nice to welcome him to the team publicly. Sort of a combination welcome and apology." She passed the notebook to Elizabeth. "I thought maybe one of these would work."

Elizabeth opened the notebook. On the first page was a cartoon of Winston. He was wearing a short cheerleading skirt, his muscular legs sticking out underneath, and above the cartoon was the caption, *Nice knees!* Under the cartoon Grace had written, *Welcome to the team, Winston!*

"Grace, this is fantastic!" Elizabeth cried. "I had no idea you were such a good artist!"

Grace blushed. "I just do it for fun. I did most of those cartoons during Boosters practice." She grinned. "With all the arguing and gossiping, there's a lot of free time."

Elizabeth looked at the other cartoons. There was one of Winston doing a cartwheel, and one showing Winston on top of a human pyramid. There was even one of Winston dressed like Superman and carrying a baton. On his chest was the label *Supercheerleader!*

"Are all these of Winston?" Elizabeth asked.

Grace blushed again. "Well, yes," she admitted.

Elizabeth smiled. "I think my favorite is the one with him in a skirt," she said. "Winston has a great sense of humor. I know he'll love it."

"Can you get it into your next issue?"

"With a little rearranging, sure," Elizabeth said. "I can't wait to see Winston's face when he sees this on the front page of the *Sixers!*"

Elizabeth pushed open the glass library doors on Monday morning and deposited a stack of *Sixers* in the box by the checkout area.

"I loved that cartoon in your paper today, Elizabeth," whispered Ms. Luster, the librarian.

"Thanks," Elizabeth said. "But Grace Oliver deserves the credit." She searched the rows of tables. "Have you seen Amy Sutton here, by any chance?"

"Why, yes, I believe she's at the table in the corner."

Elizabeth picked up a copy of the *Sixers* and headed for the corner. "I have your paper, Amy," she called. "Special delivery!"

As the table where Amy was sitting came into view, Elizabeth paused for a second. It wasn't just Amy sitting at the table—it was Amy and *Todd!* They were sitting next to each other, looking at a book, their heads bowed close together.

They both looked up from the book. "Elizabeth!" Amy said, barely suppressing a smile. "I thought you were distributing the *Sixers*."

"I *was*," Elizabeth said. "Here." She tossed Amy's copy on the table. "Sorry I didn't bring two."

Elizabeth spun on her heel and headed toward the library door, glancing behind her one last time. She knew Amy was only with Todd because of their plan. Still, she couldn't help feeling a twinge of jealousy, seeing them together.

I guess when the boy is your boyfriend and the girl is your best friend, it feels a little different, Elizabeth thought as she stepped into the hallway.

"I still say you should have gotten a Boosters vote before asking the *Sixers* to run this stupid cartoon, Grace," Janet complained at the Unicorner during lunch.

Lila examined the cover of her *Sixers* carefully. "It's not a stupid cartoon. This looks exactly like Winston, right down to his hairy legs!"

"I'm not talking about the drawing. I'm mad because it sounds like we all want to make up and be good buddies," Janet said.

"I thought it was time we apologized for everything that went on last week," Grace argued. "Look at how well things have been going since Winston joined up. His cheers are fantastic."

"It *is* a lot of fun," Tamara admitted.

"You just like it because you get to stand in front for a change," Janet muttered.

"Shh!" Tamara hissed. "Here comes Winston!"

"He probably wants to thank us," Janet said sarcastically.

Winston stood at the end of the table. Instantly Jessica recognized that something was wrong. His easy smile was gone, replaced by a grim frown, and his fists were tightly clenched.

Janet held up her hand. "You don't have to thank us, Winston—"

"I'm not here to thank you. I'm here to tell you what you all want to hear." He took a deep breath. "I quit."

The Unicorns all fell silent.

"Very funny, Winston," Jessica said at last. "You're a real comedian."

"This isn't a joke, Jessica." Winston's voice was hard. He scanned the table, his eyes dark with bitterness. "Don't look so shocked. You got what you wanted. You win."

Winston turned and walked away as the Unicorns watched in amazement.

"This is some kind of weird joke, right?" Lila asked.

"I don't think so," Kimberly said uneasily. "He looked pretty serious to me."

"I don't understand," Grace said unhappily.

"Why would Winston quit now? Things were finally working out."

"Who cares why he quit?" Janet asked. "The point is, we're rid of him." She jumped to her feet. "I'd say this calls for a celebration. Ice cream bars for everybody! And they're on me!"

Everyone cheered except Grace and Mandy. Jessica yelled along with the others, but inside she felt a little disappointed.

"What do you mean, I have to hold Lila on my shoulders?" Jessica cried indignantly at Boosters practice that afternoon.

"*Someone's* got to do it, and Winston isn't here anymore," Janet said.

"No way," Jessica said adamantly. She had been putting up with Janet's bossiness for quite a while, but this was the last straw. Suddenly she wished Winston were there to help settle this latest argument. Of course, if Winston were there, she wouldn't have to lift Lila to begin with.

"Maybe we should just forget Winston's new cheer," Amy said unhappily. "We'd have to rechoreograph the whole thing."

"But it's our best cheer!" Kimberly wailed.

"Listen up, everybody," Janet said, clapping her hands. "You're beginning to sound as if you actually *miss* Winston! Now let's start acting like the old Boosters! The championship Boosters!"

For the next half-hour the girls practiced cheer after cheer, but nothing seemed to go right. Grace was so depressed that her voice could hardly be heard. Amy complained all the way through the pyramid. And the worst part of the afternoon came when Lila fell off Jessica's shoulders—directly onto Janet. After that, Janet called off practice and sent everyone home.

As she walked through the main corridor, Jessica caught sight of Amy near the front entrance. She was leaning against the door, talking to Todd. Fortunately, her back was to Jessica. Jessica eased a little closer, tiptoeing as she went.

"I'd really appreciate a little more help with my project, Todd," Amy was saying.

Todd shrugged. "Well, sure, if you think you need it," he said, sounding a little uncomfortable. "I always thought you were a whiz at science, though."

"A little extra help never hurt," Amy replied lightly. "How about if you come by my house tomorrow afternoon and help me out?"

"Well, I guess," Todd answered. "But I still say you know more about frogs than *I* ever will!"

Jessica shook her head in amazement. Amy Sutton, Elizabeth's best friend, inviting Todd over to her house? Could Amy be planning to steal Todd from Elizabeth?

Twelve

◇

"Why do you think Winston quit the Boosters?" Elizabeth asked Jessica that night.

Jessica was in the bathroom, trying to weave purple and white ribbons into her French braid.

"*I* don't know why," Jessica said irritably. "You know Winston a lot better than I do. Why don't you ask him yourself?"

"I'm going to, first thing tomorrow," Elizabeth said. "I tried to talk to him this afternoon, but I got the feeling he was avoiding me."

Jessica turned to face Elizabeth. "Speaking of Winston," she began carefully, "how are things going with you and Todd?"

Elizabeth seemed to stiffen. "I haven't seen

much of Todd lately," she said. "I guess he's been busy."

"Busy doing what?" Jessica pressed, watching her twin carefully.

"Who knows?" Elizabeth said. She stood up abruptly. "I've got some work to do, Jess. My science project's due soon. So is yours, by the way."

And so is Amy's, Jessica thought as she watched her twin leave. Did Elizabeth suspect that something was going on between Amy and Todd? Should Jessica tell her?

And to think this all started over Winston Egbert, Jessica thought bitterly. The guy was nothing but trouble.

Elizabeth caught up with Winston the next morning as he locked his bike to the bicycle rack outside school.

"Winston, why did you quit the Boosters?" she asked.

Winston slung his backpack onto one shoulder. "Why do you think?" he asked, his voice oddly strained. "You ought to know, Elizabeth."

"Me?" Elizabeth asked. "Why?"

"You're the one who printed the Boosters' cartoon, aren't you?"

Elizabeth couldn't believe her ears. Winston sounded *angry* about the cartoon!

"It was bad enough having the Boosters ridicule me during practice," Winston continued in a rush. "But to have the entire school see Grace's cartoon—that was the last straw."

"Winston," Elizabeth said urgently, grabbing his arm, "that cartoon was meant to *welcome* you! We thought you'd love it!"

Winston gazed at Elizabeth skeptically. "You expect me to believe that?"

"It's the truth!" Elizabeth cried. They walked together for a few moments in silence. "I just don't understand why you'd quit now," Elizabeth said. "You put up with all kinds of pranks. You even put up with a black eye. Why give up now?"

Winston kicked a stone on the sidewalk. For a moment he didn't say a word. "If I tell you the truth," he said reluctantly, "you promise not to tell a soul?"

"Of course."

"The real reason I joined the Boosters wasn't because I'm dying to be a cheerleader, or because I love gymnastics so much—although it *is* a lot of fun. And it wasn't so I could make the world safe for male cheerleaders." Winston paused. "It was because of Grace Oliver. I've had this incredible crush on her as long as I can remember. I guess I thought joining the Boosters would be a good way to get to know her." He shrugged self-consciously. "You know how I am around girls."

Elizabeth smiled. "You're great around me."

"Yeah, but you're not a *girl*." Winston rolled his eyes. "I mean—you know what I mean, don't you? To me you're a friend who happens to be a girl, not a girlfriend."

Elizabeth nodded. "I know *exactly* what you mean."

"Anyway, when I saw that cartoon Grace did, I realized what a big joke she really thinks I am," Winston said sadly.

"Winston," Elizabeth said. "Please listen to me. Grace wanted to welcome you to the team, not drive you away."

"Honest?" Winston asked, his voice rising hopefully.

"Honest. As a matter of fact," Elizabeth added, "I have a feeling she thinks you're pretty great, too."

Winston broke into a dazzling smile. "You mean she realizes what a charming and lovable guy I really am? Elizabeth, this is fantastic!"

That afternoon Elizabeth stopped by Amy's house on the way home from school. She wanted to return some notes she had borrowed from her during English. Besides, if everything was going according to schedule, Todd was supposed to be there.

Mrs. Sutton answered the front door when

Elizabeth arrived. "Hi, Elizabeth," she said. "Come on in. They're in the kitchen working on Amy's science project."

Elizabeth headed to the kitchen, where she found Amy and Todd working side by side. There was a glass aquarium in the middle of the table, filled with several frogs.

Again Elizabeth felt an unexpected stab of jealousy. "Todd!" she exclaimed indignantly. "What are *you* doing here?" She had planned her lines carefully, but she found herself saying them with more force than she had intended.

"Helping Amy with her science project," Todd replied matter-of-factly. "What does it look like?"

"*I'll* tell you what it looks like!" Elizabeth fumed. "It looks like you two are more than just friends, *that's* what it looks like!"

"Elizabeth, that's ridiculous," Todd said, his voice rising slightly. He nudged Amy. "Tell her, Amy."

But Amy didn't answer. She sat at the table looking uncomfortable.

"Why don't you believe me?" Todd cried, shoving back his chair as he stood. "Amy and I are friends. She wanted help with her science project on frogs, and so I—"

"*Amy* wanted help?" Elizabeth cried, pacing

back and forth. "Amy Sutton, who got an A-plus on her last science project? Amy Sutton, who won second prize in the science fair last year?"

Todd looked like a cornered animal. "Amy!" he demanded. "Tell her, would you?"

Amy shrugged helplessly. "I've never been very good with amphibians," she said lamely.

"Todd!" Elizabeth wailed, her voice cracking. "How could you *do* this to me?"

"Do what?" Todd cried. "I haven't done anything except feed some frogs!"

Amy rushed over to a kitchen drawer and retrieved a box of tissues. "There, there, Elizabeth," Amy said, handing her a few. "Don't be upset. You and Todd weren't getting along very well, anyway."

Elizabeth blew her nose loudly.

"We were *so* getting along!" Todd cried. "Come on, Elizabeth," he begged, "please believe me!"

Elizabeth tossed aside her tissue and smiled brightly. "OK!" she said cheerfully. "I'll believe what you say about you and Amy, if you'll believe what I say about Winston and me."

Todd's mouth dropped open and he took a step backward. "Wait just a minute here," he said warily, glancing from Elizabeth's smiling face to Amy's. "You two set me up, didn't you?" He knocked his palm against his forehead. "How could I have been so stupid?" He turned to Amy. "I should have known something was up when you understood this project better than I did!"

Amy giggled.

Todd grinned sheepishly. "OK, Elizabeth," he said reluctantly. "I get it. If Amy and I can be friends, then I admit it's possible that you and Winston are just friends, too."

"I've also got something to admit," Elizabeth said. "I actually felt jealous of you and Amy, even though I knew you were just friends."

"See?" Todd said. "It's not so easy when you're on the other end of things, is it?"

"I'm sorry it had to come to this, Todd," Elizabeth said, "but I couldn't think of any other way to get through to you that you have nothing to worry about."

Todd shook his head. "Poor old Winston," he said. "He's been having a tough time lately. I guess I haven't been as much of a friend as I should have been."

"You were right about one thing, though," Elizabeth said. "Winston *can* take care of himself. I was being overprotective."

"Still, he could probably use a little moral support now," Todd replied. "I promise I'll be a better friend to Winston—*if* you promise I don't have to spend any more time with Amy's frogs!"

*   *   *

As Jessica walked home from her weekly Unicorn meeting that afternoon, she decided what she had to do. She'd agonized long enough over the situation with Amy and Todd. She had to tell Elizabeth.

She paused in the Wakefields' kitchen, trying to decide what was the best way to break the horrible news. There was no easy way to say what she had to say.

Jessica took a deep breath. "Lizzie?" she called.

"I'm in the den, Jess."

Jessica marched toward the den. "Elizabeth," she began quickly, "there's something you have to know—" Her words froze on her lips. There sat Elizabeth and Todd on the couch, like lovebirds!

"Get out of here, you—you two-timer!" Jessica cried. She reached for a pillow and tossed it as hard as she could. It glanced off Todd's head and landed on the floor.

"You big jerk!" Jessica shouted, shaking her finger in Todd's face. "You—" She paused, groping for an appropriate word.

"Jessica," Elizabeth said calmly as Jessica reached for another pillow, "it's not what you think."

"No, it's not what *you* think!" Jessica yelled. "Amy and Todd have been—"

"I know," Elizabeth interrupted, giggling. "I arranged it."

Jessica let the pillow drop to the floor. "You arranged it?"

"To teach Todd a lesson about Winston."

"B-but why didn't you tell me?" Jessica stammered.

"Because I wanted to teach *you* a lesson, too," Elizabeth explained. "Look how you jumped to the wrong conclusion, Jessica. It *is* possible for guys and girls to be just friends, you know."

For a moment, Jessica debated whether to pick up the pillow and throw it at Elizabeth. Then she smiled. "Elizabeth Wakefield," she said, "you're almost as sneaky as I am!"

Thirteen

◇

On Wednesday afternoon Winston swallowed
hard and marched across the gym. The Boosters
were standing in line doing baton drills. They had
just begun their practice, and it was obvious from
the stunned looks on their faces that they were
surprised to see him. Winston smiled at Grace,
who blushed and dropped her baton.

What's the worst they can say? Winston reminded
himself. *You're already off the squad.*

Janet stepped out of the line. "I thought you
quit," she said.

"I did," Winston replied. "But after giving it
some thought, I've decided I may have made a
mistake. I misunderstood the cartoon you put in
the *Sixers*." He looked over at Grace again. "I

didn't understand that you were just trying to welcome me to the team."

"*We* weren't trying to welcome you," Janet replied. "Grace was. She drew that cartoon without official Boosters approval."

"Speak for yourself, Janet," Amy said. "I thought it was a great idea!"

Winston cleared his throat. "Well, Ms. Langberg told me that my uniform arrived, and since I already know all the routines, it would kind of be a waste to quit now—"

"Forget it, Winston," Janet interrupted. "You already quit the squad. You can't *unquit!*"

"Why not?" Grace argued. "We need him on the team!"

"Maybe you do, Grace," Janet said. "But the rest of us don't!"

"Come on, Janet," Amy said. "Without Winston, this squad's falling apart."

Winston looked hopefully at Janet, but the look on her face told him he was fighting a losing battle. "Well, if you change your minds, you know where to find me," he said quietly, heading for the door. Before leaving, he paused. "No matter what happens, I want to wish you guys luck at the championship."

He stepped into the hallway. *At least I tried*, he told himself.

Suddenly the gym door opened and Grace

appeared. "Winston!" she called, running up to join him. "I feel so horrible about that cartoon. Elizabeth and I thought you would think it was funny. I just wanted you to feel like part of the squad."

"But I *did* feel like part of the squad, Grace," Winston replied. "Thanks to you—and Amy."

"The Boosters aren't the same without you." Grace looked down at the floor, her face growing pink.

For once in my life, Winston thought, *I'm making someone else blush!* "I'm not the same without the Boosters," he answered.

"Well, I guess I should get back to practice," Grace said. "See you later?"

"Sure," Winston replied. "Don't forget to work on that pyramid!"

As he watched Grace return to the gym, Winston wondered if he would ever get up the nerve to let her know how he really felt. He was brave, but not *that* brave.

"Would you look at this crowd?" Elizabeth cried as she and Todd stepped into the gymnasium Saturday morning.

The bleachers were already packed with spectators for the cheerleading competition. Everywhere, groups of nervous cheerleaders dressed in colorful uniforms milled about. A huge sign that the Boosters had painted hung across the far wall. WELCOME TO THE SOUTHERN CALIFORNIA MIDDLE SCHOOL CHEERING CHAMPIONSHIP! it said in large blue letters. There were a dozen blue and white balloons tied at each end of the bleachers.

"We'd better get a seat before the place fills up any more," Todd said.

"Do you see Winston anywhere?" Elizabeth asked, scanning the bleachers.

"Are you sure he's coming?"

"No, but I was hoping he might," Elizabeth replied.

"If I were him, I'd be pretty mad right now," Todd said. "Why would he want to come and root for the Boosters after the way they treated him?"

"They weren't all mean," Elizabeth reminded Todd. "Don't forget Amy and Grace."

As they found seats near the end of the bleachers, Todd pointed toward a corner of the gym. "There are the Boosters now!"

"Go Boosters!" Elizabeth yelled, but her voice was lost in the noise of the crowded gymnasium.

"Jess has been nervous all week," Elizabeth whispered. "This morning she couldn't even eat breakfast. And you know Jess—she's always hungry!"

As the five judges for the competition filed in and sat at the special table on the sideline, the crowd grew quiet. All the cheerleaders moved to the sidelines to await their turns.

"You know what's amazing?" Elizabeth said as she gazed at the colorful squads. "There are a *lot* of male cheerleaders here!"

"I'll bet almost every team has at least one guy on it," Todd agreed.

Elizabeth groaned. "Poor Winston. It's so unfair that he's not competing, too."

Ms. Langberg walked out to the microphone in the center of the gym. "Welcome to the annual Southern California Middle School Cheering Championship," she said. "It's a delight to see that so many friends and family members have come out to cheer on their teams. As most of you know, the competition is divided into two parts—a preliminary round and a final round. Scores for the two rounds are tallied to determine the overall winner of the championship."

After Ms. Langberg introduced the judges, she explained that team captains had drawn numbers from a hat to determine the order in which the squads would compete.

"And now for the first squad!" she said. "Let's have a warm welcome for the cheerleaders of John F. Kennedy Middle School in San Diego!"

"At least the Boosters weren't first," Elizabeth whispered. "Then they'd be even more nervous."

While the first squad ran through its mandatory cheer sequence, Elizabeth scoured the bleachers for a sign of Winston. He hadn't come after all, she decided.

Three more squads competed, each better than the previous one, before Ms. Langberg announced the Boosters.

Elizabeth reached for Todd's hand. "I'm so nervous, I can hardly watch!" she whispered.

The audience burst into enthusiastic applause as the Boosters dashed to the center of the gym.

"Wow, they look great—" Elizabeth began, but Lila suddenly tripped on her shoelace and landed with a thud on the shiny gym floor.

A few people in the crowd laughed while Lila picked herself up and ran to join the group, a horrified expression on her face.

"Uh-oh. Poor Lila," Elizabeth whispered.

But unfortunately for the Boosters, Lila's fall was just the beginning.

"How could you have tripped like that?" Janet asked Lila when the Boosters reached the safety of the hallway.

"Me?" Lila cried. "How could *you* have forgotten what V-I-C-T-O-R-Y spells?"

Janet slumped against the wall. "I just went blank all of a sudden."

"Thanks a lot, fearless leader," Jessica cried.

"We got the lowest score possible, do you realize that? When I walked by the judges, the one on the end told me it looked like *I* needed cheering up. Some cheerleaders we are!"

"You're one to talk!" Janet said accusingly. "You dropped your baton twice!"

"Ellen dropped hers three times!" Jessica retorted.

Ellen clutched at her heart dramatically. "Can you die of humiliation?"

"No, unfortunately," Jessica replied. "If we could, we'd all be dead, and we wouldn't have to go out for the second round and be humiliated all over again."

Inside the gym, the crowd was roaring for another squad.

"Listen to that," Kimberly moaned. "Nobody cheered when we were out there."

"A few people did," Grace said hopefully.

"They only did it out of pity, Grace," Jessica said bitterly. "And they were probably family members who were just grateful to see us leave the gym floor and stop embarrassing them."

"Well, the team out there now is coed," Janet said, pouting. "It isn't fair that we have to compete against them."

"We *could* have had a guy on our squad," Amy reminded Janet.

"How was I supposed to know that every

cheering squad in California had gone coed?"
Janet cried.

The group fell silent. "I wish Winston were
here," Grace finally said.

"Let's face it, we were a lot better when Winston was on the team," Kimberly said.

Even Janet couldn't argue.

"It's too late now," Jessica pointed out. "We're
doomed."

"Hey, guys!"

As if by magic, Winston appeared from around
the corner, smiling. "I just stopped by to wish
you luck!"

"Winston!" Amy cried. "What are you doing
here?"

"I couldn't miss the biggest competition of the
year," Winston said. "But you guys don't look too
happy."

"Didn't you see?" Grace asked.

Winston shook his head. "I just got here."

"We bombed," Jessica informed him. "Big
time."

"We set a new low in cheerleading," Amy agreed.

"I'm sure it wasn't so bad," Winston said.
"You just needed to warm up. Wait until they see
the pyramid!"

Jessica looked at Janet, who was looking at
Lila, who was looking at Kimberly. At last Janet
cleared her throat.

"Um," she began reluctantly, looking at the floor, "Winston?"

"Yes?"

"Lila has something to say to you."

Lila seemed completely stunned. "Well . . ." she said slowly, looking uncomfortable. "There's something Jessica would like to say to you."

Jessica pulled herself up straight. Why should she be the one to swallow her pride? She glanced around the group. "Grace?" she said at last.

Grace stood up and approached Winston. "Winston?"

"Yes?"

"I know this is asking a lot, and I wouldn't blame you if you never wanted to speak to us again after everything that's happened, but . . ."

"Yes?"

"Would you consider rejoining the Boosters?"

Winston smiled from ear to ear. "That's the best invitation I've had all morning," he said happily.

"So you'll do it?" Amy asked excitedly.

"You'll compete?" Jessica asked, but Winston was already dashing off down the hall.

"Where are you going?" Janet called frantically.

"You don't want me to compete in blue jeans, do you?" Winston yelled, and disappeared into the boys' locker room.

Fourteen

◇

After changing into the sweatpants and sweater Ms. Langberg had ordered for him, Winston paused to admire himself in the mirror. *I make a fine-looking cheerleader*, he thought.

Once again he replayed in his mind the moment when Grace had asked him to rejoin the squad. He was definitely a lucky guy.

Winston stepped out into the empty hallway.

"Hey, Winnie!"

Winston froze in place. He would know that voice anywhere.

Slowly he turned. It was Charlie Cashman and *three* of his oversized buddies. And they didn't look like they were there to shoot the breeze.

"Still haven't learned your lesson, have you?" Charlie said, stepping closer.

Winston stepped back against the wall, bracing himself. There was no easy way to escape, and he knew he couldn't survive a fight with these odds.

"I think we need to give you a little reminder of our earlier discussion, Winnie," Charlie sneered.

"That's *Winston* to you!"

Winston turned in the direction of the voice. *Jessica Wakefield?* he thought in amazement.

But it wasn't just Jessica. There in the hallway stood all the Boosters, hands on hips. And they looked ready for a fight.

Charlie's three friends took several steps backward. Charlie stood still, chewing nervously on his bottom lip.

"You're not afraid of a few girls, are you?" Winston said.

"Leave him alone," Jessica shouted, "or we'll make your lives miserable!"

"We'll spread so much gossip, no girl will ever go out with any of you again!" Lila added.

"Come on, Charlie," Winston said. "I'd be happy to take you on without your bodyguards."

Charlie turned, casting a pleading look at his friends.

"No, thanks," one of them replied quickly. "You already got a week of detention after word got out about the black eye you gave Winston. Next time they'll suspend you, Charlie." He shook his head. "Besides, I don't feel like messing with the Unicorns."

Charlie looked stricken. He took a nervous step backward, searching for an easy escape. "Maybe some other time," he said, trying unsuccessfully to look tough. Without another word, he turned and walked away, scurrying to catch up with his three retreating friends.

"I guess I'm braver than I thought," Winston said as he joined the girls.

"You mean taking on Charlie?" Amy asked.

"No," Winston said, laughing. "I mean taking on the Unicorns!"

Winston stood in the center of the gym, trying to catch his breath. *So far, so good*, he thought.

In fact, the Boosters had been better than good in the final round of competition. They had jumped higher and cheered louder than any of the other squads. Every routine had been flawlessly executed, and every time they finished the crowd had burst into tremendous applause.

But one thing still remained. The grand finale at the end of their last cheer—the pyramid formation.

They hadn't had much practice using the whole squad. He felt better knowing he would be spotting them, but one wrong move—one misplaced hand or foot, one careless gesture—could bring the whole thing toppling to the floor and ruin their chances.

He glanced over at the other Boosters. They were all breathless and flushed, standing nervously as they awaited Janet's signal to begin the final cheer.

"Just remember!" Winston whispered so that only the Boosters could hear, "no giggling!"

To his relief, everyone smiled. He hoped he had broken the tension just a little.

Janet and Jessica stepped forward and clapped twice in unison.

"We are the best!" the Boosters began to cheer, their voices loud and clear. "Better than the rest!"

The squad began to move into position for the pyramid. *Come on!* Winston thought as he moved to the back.

Like clockwork, the pyramid began to form. Jessica climbed effortlessly to the top and stood there confidently, arms upraised in a perfect V. Tamara and Janet stood on either side with arms outstretched.

"Go, Sweet Valley, go!" they all chanted. "Show them what you know!"

At that moment Jessica jumped off the top of the pyramid and completed a perfect midair somersault. She landed solidly on the mat, smiling triumphantly as the crowd roared its approval.

Grace looked back at Winston and flashed him a jubilant smile, and at that moment he knew all the trouble of the past couple of weeks had been worth it.

"Second place!" Jessica marveled, holding the glittering trophy high in the air. "Can you believe it?"

"If we hadn't screwed up the first round, we'd have won!" Janet said, shaking her head in amazement. "And I was sure we'd come in dead last!"

"Wait until next year!" Elizabeth said with a smile as she joined the group.

"We couldn't have done it without Winston," Grace reminded them.

"Three cheers for Winston!" Amy cried. The group broke into loud cheers.

For the first time in a while, Winston blushed. "It wasn't just me," he said modestly when the noise had died down. "It was a team effort."

Todd reached over to shake Winston's hand. "I have to say I admire you, Winston," he said.

"Thanks, Todd," Winston said happily. "Want to join up?"

Todd laughed. "Not me! I'll leave the Unicorns to you!"

Elizabeth patted Winston on the back. "I

knew you could do it,'' she said affectionately.
"Was it worth it?"

Winston smiled at Grace. "Absolutely."

Elizabeth reached for Todd's hand and pulled
him aside. "Want to see a happy ending?" she
whispered. She pointed toward Winston. He was
talking to Grace, red-faced and tongue-tied, but
that wasn't what had caught Elizabeth's attention.

Winston and Grace were also holding hands.

On Monday, the entire school was talking
about the Boosters' amazing showing at the cheering championship. Jessica basked in all the attention. It was almost like being a movie star—
except, of course, that she had to share center
stage with Winston and the rest of the Boosters.

But by the time Mr. Seigel's science class
rolled around that afternoon, the Boosters' performance was already fading from discussion, and
Jessica was already missing the limelight. She was
in no mood to hear about a bunch of boring science projects.

Amy Sutton was the first person Mr. Seigel
called on. Jessica yawned as Amy carried a large
plastic aquarium up to the front of the classroom.
"How thrilling," Jessica whispered to Lila, who
was sitting in front of her. "There's nothing I like
better than slimy—"

Suddenly Amy lost her grip on the aquarium,

and it dropped to the floor with a loud thud. Amy gasped as the wire top came loose and a dozen frogs made a mad dash for freedom.

"Grab them!" Amy screamed as students leaped from their chairs.

"Gross!" Lila groaned. "No way am I touching one of those things!"

"Give Amy a hand, class," Mr. Seigel said just as a large bullfrog flew onto his desk.

Todd Wilkins lunged toward the front of the room. "Gotcha, Barney!" he cried. He held the frog up for Amy to see.

While the rest of the class bounced around the room trying to locate frogs, Jessica and Lila stayed in their seats, watching calmly. "You know what I wish?" Jessica mused as a small green member of Amy's project leaped over her backpack. "I wish I had a camera to take a picture of this."

"Better yet, a camcorder," Lila agreed.

"There's a frog in my blouse!" Ellen Riteman screamed frantically, dashing over to Amy. Jessica laughed as Ellen wriggled wildly, trying to dislodge the frog.

"I'm still missing one frog," Amy said to the class. "Her name is Wilma. Would you all mind looking a little longer?"

Jessica shifted in her chair and heard a loud, angry croak.

"Jess," Lila said, "I could be wrong, but I think you're sitting on Wilma."

Jessica leaped from her chair to find a very small, very cranky frog on the edge of the seat. Reluctantly she picked up the frog with two fingers and daintily carried her over to Amy.

"Jessica's found Wilma!" Amy announced happily.

The class broke into enthusiastic applause, and Jessica took a little bow. *What a wonderful sound*, she thought.

Will Jessica find stardom? Find out in Sweet Valley Twins and Friends #53, **THE SLIME THAT ATE SWEET VALLEY**

The most exciting story ever in Sweet Valley history

FRANCINE PASCAL'S

SWEET VALLEY Saga

THE SWEET VALLEY SAGA tells the incredible story of the lives and times of five generations of brave and beautiful young women who were Jessica and Elizabeth's ancestors. Their story is the story of America: from the danger of the pioneering days to the glamour of the roaring nineties, the sacrifice and romance of World War II to the rebelliousness of the Sixties, right up to the present-day Sweet Valley. A dazzling novel of unforgettable lives and love both lost and won, THE SWEET VALLEY SAGA is Francine Pascal's most memorable, exciting, and wonderful Sweet Valley book ever.

BANTAM

NEW YORK ● TORONTO ● LONDON ● SYDNEY ● AUCKLAND

☐	15681-0	**TEAMWORK #27**	**$2.75**
☐	15688-8	**APRIL FOOL! #28**	**$2.75**
☐	15695-0	**JESSICA AND THE BRAT ATTACK #29**	**$2.75**
☐	15715-9	**PRINCESS ELIZABETH #30**	**$2.95**
☐	15727-2	**JESSICA'S BAD IDEA #31**	**$2.75**
☐	15747-7	**JESSICA ON STAGE #32**	**$2.99**
☐	15753-1	**ELIZABETH'S NEW HERO #33**	**$2.99**
☐	15766-3	**JESSICA, THE ROCK STAR #34**	**$2.99**
☐	15772-8	**AMY'S PEN PAL #35**	**$2.95**
☐	15778-7	**MARY IS MISSING #36**	**$2.99**
☐	15779-5	**THE WAR BETWEEN THE TWINS #37**	**$2.99**
☐	15789-2	**LOIS STRIKES BACK #38**	**$2.99**
☐	15798-1	**JESSICA AND THE MONEY MIX-UP #39**	**$2.95**
☐	15806-6	**DANNY MEANS TROUBLE #40**	**$2.99**
☐	15810-4	**THE TWINS GET CAUGHT #41**	**$2.99**
☐	15824-4	**JESSICA'S SECRET #42**	**$2.95**
☐	15835-X	**ELIZABETH'S FIRST KISS #43**	**$2.95**
☐	15837-6	**AMY MOVES IN #44**	**$2.95**
☐	15843-0	**LUCY TAKES THE REINS #45**	**$2.99**
☐	15849-X	**MADEMOISELLE JESSICA #46**	**$2.95**
☐	15869-4	**JESSICA'S NEW LOOK #47**	**$2.95**
☐	15880-5	**MANDY MILLER FIGHTS BACK #48**	**$2.99**
☐	15899-6	**THE TWINS' LITTLE SISTER #49**	**$2.99**
☐	15911-9	**JESSICA AND THE SECRET STAR #50**	**$2.99**

Bantam Books, Dept. SVT5, 414 East Golf Road, Des Plaines, IL 60016

Please send me the items I have checked above. I am enclosing $_____ (please add $2.50 to cover postage and handling). Send check or money order, no cash or C.O.D.s please.

Mr/Ms _____

Address _____

City/State _____ Zip _____

Please allow four to six weeks for delivery.
Prices and availability subject to change without notice.

SVT5-9/91